XONARYE

S. H. S.

Disclaimer:
This is a work of fiction. All characters, locations, and businesses are purely products of the author's imagination and are entirely fictitious. Any resemblance to actual people, living or dead, or to businesses, places, or events is completely coincidental.

ONE

Leaf stood there for a few moments, trying to figure out if he had actually seen that tattoo. Then he turned and started walking down the tunnel towards the plane, when something else jumped into his mind.

He stopped flat footed and yelled out to Selina, "Selina Delacruise doesn't sound like a Kosovan name. It sounds more like Spanish or Portuguese. Also, your accent doesn't sound right either."

Selina and Spence both stopped and looked back at him, and Selina gave him a slight smile. "I was waiting for one of you two to twig," she answered.

"Where are you from then?" asked Leaf. "I need to know or I am not going on the plane with you. I need to trust the people I am with."

"I like your style," she responded. "Trust is severely underrated in this day and age."

"You're not answering my question," said Leaf, starting to get annoyed.

"I am from Kosovo," replied Selina. "However, I grew up in Spain. My parents died when I was a baby, and a Spanish couple adopted me and raised me as their daughter. How's that for trust? Now, get your arse on the plane before I drag it on!" she yelled out, turning around and making her way towards the plane door.

"Smooth move, Leaf," said Spence as Leaf caught up to his mate. "What a way to piss off the person who is supposed to be protecting us."

"I needed to know who I am dealing with for our own safety," replied Leaf. "Plus, mate, if we build a bond with her, she is more likely to look after us," he added.

Spence looked surprised by Leaf's comments. "I am not just a pretty face," said Leaf with a wink, while giving his friend a high five.

Just then, the stewardess came up the tunnel towards them. She didn't look very happy. "Gentleman, we are all waiting for you to board so we can leave. If you would kindly make your way to your seats now, thank you," she said in an aggravated voice.

The boys looked at each other skittishly and hastily made their way aboard.

At last, Leaf was in his seat by the window, ready to take off, while Selina and Spence were scattered in different rows elsewhere. Leaf was sitting next to an elderly lady in her sixties, with thick glasses and curly grey hair. She was obviously hard of hearing too, judging by the way she loudly spoke to the stewardess in her thick Southern American accent.

Oh boy, Leaf thought, as if the trip wasn't going to be long enough without having to sit next to a deaf elderly lady.

Fortunately, his prayers were answered when a stewardess came up and explained to the lady that she had been upgraded to first class free of charge. Leaf could have done a dance on his seat before he realised who was coming to take her place.

It was Selina, and she looked pissed at him. It was written all over her face. She grabbed the two cords of his hoodie, and before he knew what was going on, she was choking him with them.

Selina leaned across to his ear and whispered, "If you ever pull a stunt like that again, I will kill you myself. Now, just nod if you understand."

Leaf nodded his head slowly while desperately trying to breathe, as Selina slowly released the cords from her grasp. Leaf started gasping for air as he suddenly wondered just how deadly Selina could be.

"Are you bloody crazy? You are supposed to be here to protect us!" spluttered out Leaf at last, just about managing to catch his breath. Selina looked him straight in the eyes, and calmly stated, "Get this straight in your mind: I am not bloody crazy, and I am here to protect you and you alone."

"What do you mean?" asked Leaf, caught unaware by her statement.

"Come on, you're a smart man," Selina followed up.

"Originally, I was the only one coming, so you were only paid to protect me," confirmed Leaf.

"Well done. You finally got there," said Selina in a sarcastic tone.

"Spence is in this with me, and I am telling you that you will have to protect him," demanded Leaf.

Selina burst out laughing. "You are telling me what to do now? I guess you aren't aware yet that I only have one boss in this world and that is money. Are you sure you can afford me?" asked Selina.

Leaf smiled back at her cooly. "Never judge a book by its cover," he replied.

Selina stopped laughing, suddenly switching to an intrigued expression.

"What are they paying you to protect me?" enquired Leaf.

"Twenty thousand dollars gets your friend the same protection as you," explained Selina.

"What if something happens to him, do I get a refund?" asked Leaf with a cocky smile, but Selina just smiled right back.

"Nothing has ever happened to someone I have protected, and I don't see that changing anytime soon." She handed him a piece of paper with her bank account details. "You can put the money in there," she explained.

Leaf started making the transfer on his phone, when one of the stewardesses came up to him. "Sir, can you please turn your phone off or put it on aeroplane mode? We are about to take off."

"I guess I will have to pay you the money when we land," said Leaf.

"Let's hope nothing happens to your friend while we are up in the air then," replied Selina with a sly grin.

The plane's engines roared to life as it headed up the runway and slowly lifted off into the clear blue sky. It was the beginning of a fourteen-and-a-half hour journey that would take them across the Pacific to Santiago, Chile.

Leaf spent the first hour looking out of the window, taking in the views of the sky and the beautiful blue ocean beneath them.

Eventually, he turned around to see what Selina was doing and discovered her listening to something on her headphones. He waved his hands in front of her face to get her attention, and she slowly turned her head towards him, taking her headphones off even more slowly.

"Don't wave your hands in front of me again unless you want them broken," said Selina, looking very aggravated.

"I just wanted to get your attention," said leaf.

"Then talk to me like a normal adult does, rather than acting like a small child," responded Selina.

"Once I pay you the money to protect Spence, will you talk to me nicely?" asked Leaf, clearly not allowing himself to be intimidated by the woman.

She just gave him a half smile with the corner of her mouth. "What was it you wanted?" she asked.

"How do you think Tamina tracked us down?" he replied.

"There are many ways she could have managed that. In any case, it is quite clear that she is very intelligent, and your plans will need to change once we land in Cuba," explained Selina.

She could tell that Leaf had follow-up questions, so she got in first. "This Tamina obviously knows both of your names, what you look like, and where you are going. She will soon find out where you are staying in Chile, and that you are going to Cuba first as well," continued Selina.

Leaf was taking this all in and was about to ask another question, when Selina interrupted him. "I have cancelled the flights and accommodation in Cuba."

"When did that happen?" asked Leaf.

"When you said you saw Tamina at the airport. I went looking for her, while quickly cancelling everything on my mobile," answered Selina.

"Looks like you will be worth the money you are getting paid," saif Leaf with an impressed smile.

"I am one of the best in the world at protecting people, so don't underestimate me and what I am capable of," said Selina sternly as they relaxed back into their seats to enjoy the rest of the flight.

TWO

"If everything has been cancelled, then you must have a plan to get us to Cuba safely?" questioned Leaf.

"Yes, I have a plan to get us there," replied Selina swiftly.

"Are you going to share that plan with me?" enquired Leaf.

Selina suddenly got up out of her seat.

"Where are you going?" asked Leaf.

"I am going to the toilet if that's okay with you," responded Selina. Leaf was not happy that she had seemingly just fobbed him off, but he had no choice but to wait patiently for her to return. He was just about to go looking for her, when Spence sat down next to him unexpectedly.

"Hey mate. Selina sent me up here to cheer you up. She said you were getting grumpy," said Spence.

"Grumpy!" spat out Leaf. "She is being unreasonable and will not tell me what's going on."

"What do you mean?" questioned Spence, looking quite puzzled by the situation.

"Where do I start?" said Leaf in a huff. "Well, I got some answers, but not all the ones I wanted. Selina is here to protect me and me alone."

Spence looked surprised. "What about me?" he said worriedly.

"Don't stress mate, I am paying for your protection as soon as we touch down," explained Leaf.

"What about now, while where on the plane?" said Spence, looking even more worried now. "Come on mate, we are on a plane. We are safe here," said Leaf, trying to convince his friend that everything would be fine.

"There is a more pressing issue—" Leaf went on, but before he could finish his sentence, Spence cut him off. "What the hell is more pressing than my life?" he said, obviously quite annoyed by what Leaf had just said.

"I didn't mean it like that, Spence. Don't worry, you are perfectly safe mate," replied Leaf, trying to calm him down.

Spence just sat there looking pissed, clearly unmoved by his words. "No wonder Selina wanted to get away from you," he snorted.

"She wanted to get away because she cancelled all our flights and accommodations and wouldn't give me an answer about how she intends to get us to Cuba," said Leaf in a gruff voice.

Spence just looked at Leaf for a moment. "What do you mean she cancelled everything?" he said, suddenly forgetting how annoyed he was at Leaf, and now feeling the same towards Selina instead.

"She cancelled it all when she went looking for Tamina at the airport," explained Leaf.

"Why wouldn't she tell you?" asked Spence.

"I don't know, but I am going to get some answers," said Leaf, standing up. "Where's your seat mate?" he added.

"Right down the end of the plane on the right. It's an aisle seat."

"I will be back with shortly," proclaimed Leaf, making his way down the aisle. When he arrived at the seat, however, it was empty. Where had she gotten to, he wondered.

"Excuse me, sir," he said to the gentleman by the window. "Do you know where the lady is that was sitting in this seat?"

The gentleman looked over in surprise, slightly irritated by Leaf's question. "I don't know where she is, and this is a flight, not a bloody game of musical chairs," he responded angrily.

"I am sorry to bother you, sir. I will send back the other guy and there will be no more disturbances," said Leaf apologetically, taken aback by the man's bad attitude.

No response was forthcoming, as Leaf made his way back to his seat, where Spence was waiting for him.

"That was quick," stated Spence.

"She wasn't there, and the guy next to the window was not impressed with me being there at all," explained Leaf. "I think you better get back there before he blows a gasket."

"Yeah, all right mate, I will see you on the ground," replied Spence.

Leaf waited for what felt like hours for Selina to return and eventually fell off to sleep in his chair. Sometime later, he woke up, and as his eyes adjusted to the light above him, he soon realised that she was back in the seat next to him.

"How was your sleep, sleeping beauty?" she jeered.

Where have you been?" asked Leaf, still half asleep.

"Someone had to check the plane to make sure it was safe. Did you even stop to think about that?" asked Selina.

Of course, the thought hadn't crossed Leaf's mind at all.

"Anything could have happened to you while you slept," Selina followed up.

Leaf decided to use a different tack with her this time. "Thank you for doing that, Selina," he said sincerely.

Selina was taken aback by this response.

"How much longer before we land?" added Leaf.

"Umm, about three hours," replied Selina, still in a bit of shock from the way he was acting.

"You probably haven't slept at all. Do you want to get some now?" asked Leaf.

"All right, what are you playing at?" demanded Selina, starting to be suspicious of his new approach.

"Nothing," said Leaf. "But if we are going to be spending a lot of time together, maybe we need to get along."

Selina smiled at him in surprise. She was clearly a woman who did not like being controlled.

"In that case, we can swap seats and I will get some shut eye before we land," she said, as they changed seats so that he was in the aisle and she was by the window. It wasn't long before Selina was out for the count, with her head resting against the window.

Now with a bit of time to spare, Leaf got out his book. He wanted to go back over what he had read, just in case he missed something the first time around. He read up on the capital city, the other major cities, the currency, the economic profile, Xped, Reblick, the languages, the land mass, and the general history of Xonarye.

It was then that he discovered he had missed the part about the population. This was pretty confronting to read seeing as there were only twenty-six survivors from a place that had a total land mass of 410,000 square kilometres. He felt queasy discovering just how many people had perished during the terrible plague.

Suddenly, the plane started shaking around in the sky, and the captain's voice came through the loudspeaker. "Please fasten your seatbelt's ladies and gentlemen, we are currently experiencing some turbulence. We will let you know when it has subsided."

Leaf turned to wake Selina up and let her know about the turbulence, however she was already sitting up and strapped in. "You don't look so good," she said. "Are you feeling, okay?"

"I am just not a fan of flying, let alone turbulence," answered Leaf, who was feeling very sick, not just from the plane shuddering, but from thinking about how many people from Xonarye had passed away.

THREE

Leaf was strapped into his seat with his hands firmly gripping the armrests, trying his damnedest not to be sick while the plane shook violently. After about half an hour of rattling around like a rag doll, where on more than one occasion he was sure the plane was going to drop out of the sky like a lead balloon, the turbulence finally subsided.

"Well, that was a bit of excitement," said Selina with a sly grin at Leaf, who was looking very pale. Leaf finally gave in to his body's will, and he grabbed a sick bag and threw up in it. After he was done, he looked up at Selina, who simply said, "That wasn't so bad. I didn't feel a thing."

Leaf wished he could tell her it was not just the turbulence that had caused him to feel unwell, but he wasn't sure if he could fully trust her yet. After all, she only seemed to be interested in his money.

He stood up.

"Where are you going?" asked Selina.

"To check on Spence and go to the toilet if you must know," answered Leaf, walking up the aisle until he could make out Spence glued to his seat. He didn't look so hot either.

Leaf walked up to his friend, asking, "How are you going there mate?"

"I have been better," he responded.

"You have looked better, too," joked Leaf with a big smile, while looking over at the grumpy gentleman.

"How has he been?" he added.

"Been asleep most of the time so it's been good. How has it been with Selina?" questioned Spence.

"I have slept, she has slept. I've been sick actually, so I haven't really had a chance to get any more answers yet. I have a feeling that I will not get any until we land either," answered Leaf."

"Why do you say that?" asked Spence, looking slightly surprised.

"She doesn't like to be told what to do or be controlled in any way, shape, or form," responded Leaf.

"Do you trust her?" asked Spence.

"I trust her to protect us because she is getting paid for it," answered Leaf. "But I don't trust her enough to tell her about Xonarye. Look, I need to go to the toilet. I will see you when we are on the tarmac."

"Sounds like we have a rough plan," replied Spence.

As Leaf arrived back at his seat, Selina was still sitting there by the window where he had left her.

"How is your friend?" she asked.

"He is okay. He looks a little pale from the turbulence but nothing serious," said Leaf.

"What about the guy in the seat next to him?" asked Selina.

"He was fast asleep," answered Leaf. "Why do you ask?"

She smiled. "Good, those sleeping tablets must have kicked in."

"Sleeping tablets, really?" said Leaf, looking shocked.

"Yeah, there was something I didn't like about him, and he was grumpy as hell," replied Selina.

"If I was grumpy, would you do that to me too?" asked Leaf.

"Depends on how grumpy you get." Selina winked and Leaf was still unsure how to take her mannerisms.

The captain's voice came over the loudspeaker. "We will be landing shortly, so please make sure your seatbelts are secure."

The plane slowly made its descent from the sky, until the wheels finally screeched loudly against the bitumen's surface. Then they taxied around until they came to a stop at the airport terminal.

"Stay with Spence, go to the baggage area, get your gear, and I will meet you at the taxi rink," said Selina.

Leaf nodded his head in agreement.

"Oh, and don't forget to pay me the money to protect your friend," Selina followed up. There was that mercenary side of her again that Leaf wondered if he could truly trust.

Leaf made his way out of the plane and caught up with Spence just as they came into the terminal. There were people scooting around everywhere, but there wasn't the same hustle and bustle you'd find in Adelaide or Brisbane, as everyone had a much more relaxed vibe about them.

They both had their heads on the swivel, trying to take in all the new sights and sounds around them. The different people, the clothes, the language, the sights, the smells… and this was only the airport. The two mates just looked at each other and smiled knowingly, as they moved through the sea of people and made their way to the baggage area, where they grabbed their bags off the carousel.

Outside at the taxi rink and their heads were no longer in swivel mode, but rather full-on turning in an almost impossible manner. Leaf put his hand on Spence's shoulder and said, "I am glad you're here, mate, so I can have this experience with you."

"Yeah, me too, mate," responded Spence. "How cool would it be if Summo were here as well?" he added. Just then, they heard a familiar voice from behind them, and they both turned around to see where it came from.

OMG it was Summo! Both of their jaws dropped like kids' cartoon characters. They couldn't believe he was standing there right in front of them. Summo, for his part, had his phone out, and he was trying to take as many photos as humanly possible.

"How cool is this place?" said Summo. "My Facebook friends will love these photos."

Spence and Leaf wrapped their arms around Summo and gave him a massive hug. "What are you doing here?" said Spence excitedly.

"Well, I decided I needed to come and keep an eye on both of you," said Summo. "Plus, who else would be the brains of the operation anyway?"

Leaf and Spence burst out laughing with the last part of his sentence, as they both knew that thinking wasn't his strong point.

"Who is this guy?" came a voice from out of nowhere. It was Selina, of course.

"This is our mate, Summo," said Spence.

"Summo, this is Selina, our protection for the trip," introduced Leaf.

"Um, I think you have that wording wrong," explained Selina. "I am only getting paid to protect Leaf. You know my price for protection," she continued. "All there is here as far as I am concerned is another liability until I see some more cash."

"Bloody hell, isn't she blunt and direct," said Summo.

"No," explained Leaf, "she only cares about one thing, and that's money."

"Everyone has a price," Selina snapped back.

Leaf got out his phone and transferred the money over to the account details she had given him on the plane. "There you go. Now you have your money for both my mates too. Just remember that they are people, not just dollars and cents," said Leaf in an angry voice.

"To me, it's all business, and business is all about money," said Selina. "If I don't treat it like business, someone or something will go wrong, and that won't be very good for my reputation."

That was when the penny finally dropped for Leaf. Now he really understood what made Selina tick. This was about keeping her reputation intact, and that's why she took everything so damn seriously.

FOUR

"Anyway, Summo, why did you really decide to come and not even tell us?" asked Spence, who knew that his friend was just mucking around earlier with his reply.

"I decided that these opportunities only come around once in a lifetime and I would regret not coming," explained Summo. "Plus, I just had to see the shock on you boys' faces." He gave them a wink.

"What about your job?" asked Leaf.

"I realised that it's only a job. I can always get another one," said Summo with a smile.

"Well, this is all very touching. I wish I had a tissue to hand you guys," said Selina sarcastically with her hands on her hips. "But, we need to get out of here in case your friend from Brisbane airport is here."

A very black taxi pulled up in front of them and the guys all looked at each other. This was one of the many things that was going to be quite different for them. Being from the countryside, they hadn't been exposed to much of the world yet in their young lives, and they were used to seeing predominately white taxis, if at all.

All four of them quickly piled into the taxi and came face to face with the driver, who was an older man with brown curly hair coming out from beneath his white hat. His skin was light brown, almost leathery looking, with many wrinkles across his weathered face.

He rattled out a heap of words that none of the guys understood, and they just sat there, looking at him like a bunch of stunned mullets. Selina looked at them and shook her head, wondering what on earth she had signed up for, as Leaf pulled out his phone to use the linguist app.

Before he had a chance to speak, however, Selina was already talking to the man in fluent Spanish. The driver looked at her and smiled, then looked at the guys in the back and started laughing at them.

"What did you tell him?" snapped Summo.

"She told me you are not very bright coming to a Spanish-speaking country and not knowing a word of the language," said the diver in English while laughing heartily.

The three looked rather sheepishly at each other.

"Where are you going to?" asked the driver.

"Ask the lady; she is in charge," said Leaf, who had managed to gather his composure after feeling rather stupid about the language barrier incident only moments earlier. Selina nodded at Leaf as a sign of approval. "Can we please go to Mercado Central de Santiago," she said.

They had left Australia at 12 o'clock in the afternoon and they had gone back a day, with the local time currently just before 12 again.

The boys were staring out of the window, taking in all the sights of the city as the taxi made its way to its destination.

"What is Mercado Central de Santiago," asked Spence anxiously.

"We are going to the city's biggest market, which is also one of the biggest markets in the world," answered Selina.

"Why?" followed up Spence.

"Don't you ask a lot of questions," snorted Selina, getting a bit annoyed.

"I would like to know what is going on, seeing as we are paying for your services," responded Spence.

Selina raised her left eyebrow and looked disapprovingly at him. "And how much did you pay exactly?" she asked sternly.

There was no response, and Selina smiled, looking happy in the knowledge that she had put him back in his box.

Leaf made a loud noise, clearing his throat to get her attention, and she turned and looked at him as if her eyes would pierce straight through him. Leaf gazed back at her, trying not to be intimidated.

"How about you answer my mate's question?" said Leaf defiantly. You could cut the tension in the taxi with a knife. After a brief stare down, Selina finally responded, "There will be thousands of people there during the middle of the day, and if there is anyone following us, we will lose them in the sea of bodies." Her gaze turned back towards Spence. "Do you want to know what blood type I am as well?" she said in a huffy voice.

Summo shouted, "Time out! You know we are all on the same side here." Again, there was nothing but silence in the taxi, as the driver muttered something under his breath in Spanish. Selina responded to him in Spanish too, and then Leaf spoke up. "No, we are not related."

Selina snapped her head around from the front seat to find Leaf holding his phone open on the linguistic app. He just smiled back at her.

"Have you seen how modern looking the city is? I wasn't expecting this," said Spence in amazement.

"We have what you call new parts of the city and older parts," said the taxi driver in the best English possible.

"How long have you been a taxi driver?" followed up Spence, who had a thirst to learn and always felt the best way was to ask as many questions as possible.

"Me, ah… it would be what we call *venite*," he responded.

"*Venite*," repeated Spence in his best Spanish accent.

Summo cracked up laughing at his mate's effort.

Leaf was still playing with his phone as he said, "*Venite* is twenty in Spanish."

"Wow, that's a long time," said Summo, "we aren't even twenty years old." You could tell Spence's mind was mulling over the next question to ask, and it wasn't long before he came out with, "What is your name, *senor*?"

The driver smiled at him and you could tell he liked the attention Spence was giving him. "My name is *Senor* Jorge Garcia. I have a wife, three kids, and four grandkids," said Jorge proudly.

Spence smiled back at Jorge, while Leaf watched Selina closely from the back seat. She had been tapping away on her phone for a few minutes. She stopped what she was doing, looked around, and stared at Leaf as if she knew he had been watching her the whole time. "You know I am here to protect you, right?" she said, slightly annoyed.

"Yeah, I know," responded Leaf calmly. The two of them seemed to be at each other's throats constantly.

"Here we are, *senores* and *senorita*," said Jorge politely, pulling up the car.

FIVE

Climbing out of the cab, the three young men stood there staring at Mercado Central de Santiago. It was nothing like anyone of them had seen before in their short lives. It had a massive domed tower on top of the structure, flanked by some smaller two-tier roof buildings.

The front entrance was an archway with cast iron carvings on top of the massive opening, and there were smaller entrances that mirrored the main one as entry points to the established shops. While the lads were gawking at the massive marketplace, Selina had been back at the taxi in deep conversation with Jorge.

Eventually, she strolled past the three guys and said, "So, are we going to make a move inside or just wait for someone to spot us?"

They looked at each other and quickly shuffled after her into the giant structure. Inside, they found themselves surrounded by hundreds of different stalls in every direction. Leaf looked up at the elaborate wrought iron celling that twisted and wrapped its way all along the building, and he was mesmerised by the design and how complex the engineering looked.

Once he turned his gaze from the roof back to the others, he realised they had disappeared into the maze of market stands and people.

He spun around a few times, trying to find where his friends had ducked off to, when he felt a slight tap on his right shoulder. To his surprise, he saw Summo and Spence standing there in straw hats and woollen ponchos. They were having a laugh between themselves at his expense.

"What's so funny?" asked Leaf.

"The look on your face when you thought you were lost," said Summo.

"You think I look funny? Have you seen the outfits you two are wearing?" answered Leaf.

"Hurry up Leaf, you're next," came Selina's voice from one of the nearby stalls. She was in a similar outfit to Spence and Summo.

Leaf wandered over to Selina and asked, "What is that you are wearing and why?"

"How dense are you?" responded Selina.

"No need to be rude," retorted Leaf.

"You need to use your head and think about what is going on," said Selina. "You are being followed by someone, so you need to change your clothes and blend in," she continued.

Leaf put a poncho and hat on that matched the others.

"Before you ask your next question, stop and think. You might already know the answer," said Selina.

Leaf stood there, pondering his response, while Summo took pictures of them in their new outfits. "We came into a crowded area to change because it would be almost impossible for us to be followed," said Leaf.

"We need to keep moving. Jorge is waiting for us at the other side of the market," said Selina.

"Is that what you were talking about in the taxi?" asked Spence.

"Not much gets by you, does it?" said Selina, smiling at him.

"You should take more after him," she added, looking at Leaf.

"Stop it," said Leaf loudly as they were about to move off.

"We need to get rid of our phones as they could get tracked," added Leaf.

"We will," said Selina. "But we will do it right in the middle of the market, so it doesn't give away which exit we use."

Moving their way past the mobs of people, and what seemed like every second stall selling some sort of fresh food, they came to the middle of Mercado Central de Santiago.

"We need to leave our phones here now," instructed Selina.

The guys took their phones out and their fingers started tapping away on them.

"What are you doing?" asked Selina, looking quite annoyed at them.

"We need to save everything on our phones to the cloud," replied Summo.

Selina did not look impressed.

"Do you know how much of my life is on here? It's important to back it up to the cloud," Summo added, as the three of them finished up and tossed their phones into the closest bin.

Leaf kept the phone Frank had given him though, feeling it would be a good idea.

"What about your phone?" asked Spence, looking at Selina.

"Mine?" She smiled. "Do you think someone in my line of work would have a phone that can be tracked?"

"She's got you there," said Summo, elbowing Spence in the ribs.

"I need food before we go any further," groaned Summo.

"Good idea. I am feeling quite peckish as well," said Spence.

They looked at Selina, expecting her to be annoyed with them, but to their shock, she responded with, "Wait here and I will be back with something."

"What do you think she will come back with?" asked Summo.

"I don't know," answered Leaf. "Chilean cuisine is not one of my strong suits."

"I just hope it's not something that has too much spice in it," said Spence with a worried look on his face.

SIX

Selina returned, and to their amazement she was carrying something resembling pasties.

"How did you find pasties here?" asked Summo.

"They're not pasties," answered Selina. "They are empanadas."

"What are empanadas?" Summo followed up. He had been quite excited to try something new up until now, but he was looking quite sceptical about the food she had brought back with her.

"They are a traditional fried pastry that is filled with cheese, seafood, or beef," explained Selina.

"What are these empanadas filled with, and are they spicy?" asked Spence.

"Seafood. And no, they are not spicy," answered Selina. "Now, hurry and eat. We need to keep moving," she snapped.

Leaf, Selina, and Spence started munching away at their food, while Summo looked rather hesitant.

"This is great," remarked Spence.

"I know," said Leaf. "I could have another one after this."

Summo had still not touched his yet.

"It's not poison; it's only something new," said Spence in Summo's direction.

"You're the one who decided to come in the end because you didn't want to miss out on this adventure," Leaf reminded him.

Finally, Summo picked up the empanada, took a bite out of it, and his face turned from a terrified expression into a huge smile.

"Happy now?" asked Leaf.

"Oh yeah, this is fantastic," mumbled Summo as he munched away on the rest of his empanada.

After finishing up each of their respective empanadas, it was time to get going to their rendezvous point with Jorge at the exit.

As they moved through the market, Summo's eyes were darting around, looking at the different stalls to see what else he could grab to eat on the way out.

His eyes caught something on one of the stalls. It was inside long brown corn leaves tied up with some twine in a small package.

"Stop guys!" called Summo. "I want to try this," he said, pointing at the item on the stall.

"What?" called back Spence. "Are you serious?"

Selina was the last to hear Summo calling out to them, and she spun around and stormed back towards him.

Summo's eyes quickly turned from excitement to fear of the unknown as he saw Selina coming towards him. He wanted to move, but his shoes suddenly felt like they had been glued to the floor.

Selina stopped in front of him, leaned towards his ear, and whispered, "You better keep moving or I am going to tie you up like a pretzel."

Summo had always seen himself as something of a ladies' man, but he had never been spoken to by one like that before. He just stood there, limp, looking blankly back at her.

"This is the moment where you quickly follow the rest of us," said Selina in a calm voice with a smile on her face.

Summo slowly nodded his head and moved forward, finally lifting his once glued shoes off the floor. The other two guys watched in amazement at what transpired in front of their eyes with their mate.

On her way past, Selina stopped in front of Leaf and Spence, and said in a very authoritarian manner, "When I say it's time to move, it's time to move."

They continued walking through the multitude of people, following

Selina this way and that towards the exit. The three mates were having trouble keeping up with her because the ponchos they were wearing were hard to move around in, and the hats kept flipping and flopping in front of their vison.

Finally coming out of the humongous marketplace, they could feel the warmth of the sun and a cool breeze on them that was previously absent, as they heard a familiar voice calling out. "*Amigos, amigos*, over here, my *amigos*." It was Jorge, standing in front of his taxi, waiting for them.

"*Gracias* Jorge," said Selina with a warming smile, as they filed into the taxi, removing their straw hats so they could fit in easier.

"Your ponchos and chupallas look very good on you," said Jorge with a grin.

"What are chuppallas?" questioned Spence.

Jorge pointed to his straw hat. "Ch… ch… chuppallas," stammered out Spence, trying to repeat what Jorge had said.

Once they were all inside, a mobile phone started ringing. It was Selina's.

"What did you find out?" she immediately asked upon answering. "Yes, thank you. The money will be in your account shortly."

"What was that about?" enquired Leaf when she hung up.

"That was one of my contacts. They have been at the hotel you originally booked to check if anyone has been enquiring about you and Spence," explained Selina. "On to the airport please Jorge," she instructed.

"Back to the airport already?" exclaimed Summo.

"Yes, we need to keep on the move, and that means getting to Cuba sooner rather than later," eluded Selina.

Going back to the airport seemed like a drag to the three mates, as it had already been a bloody long day for them.

Suddenly, Summo started giggling to himself. "What's so funny?" queried Spence.

"Well, neither of you have noticed that the taxi is on a different side of the road," explained Summo.

"Only you would notice that," said Spence.

"Well, at least he is taking in his surroundings," intruded Selina.

"Now take off your ponchos and hats and leave them here in the taxi."

Doing as they were told, they placed the clothing in a pile on the back seat. "These are for you and your family, Jorge," proclaimed Selina.

"Thank you for your services," said Leaf happily.

"Yes, thank you," repeated Summo and Spence with cheerful smiles on their faces.

"Oh, *gracias, gracias, amigos*," said Jorge with great joy in his voice. You could tell from his reaction that he was grateful. Leaf placed some money inside his chuppalla as an extra thank you for his help.

As they approached the entrance to the airport, Selina moved closer to Leaf. "I saw what you did there. You know you can't be mister nice guy along the way," she scolded. Leaf mulled this over for a few seconds and just smiled back as a sign that he understood her words of advice.

Next, they ran the gauntlet of doing everything that was required to get to the boarding area of the airport, so they could catch a plane destined for Havana, Cuba.

In the boarding area, they all sat down together, and Selina started rummaging through her backpack for something. She eventually drew out three assorted hats and said, "Put these on."

Summo grabbed a black tucker cap with the Chilean flag on it and announced, "This is the most stylish one."

"Trust you to always think about you own appearance," said Spence.

Leaf picked out a blue and white national football team baseball cap, with three silhouettes of players kicking a ball.

"Oh, I didn't see that coming at all," said Spence sarcastically.

"What do you me?" retorted Leaf.

"Come on mate, you are mister sports after all," answered Summo. "I don't think there is a sport in the world you haven't seen on TV."

"Yeah, I guess so," said Leaf, putting the hat on his noggin.

That left a red bucket hat with 'Chile' in block letters coloured in white and blue for Spence, who wasn't fussed about it at all.

SEVEN

They all sat there patiently waiting to board the plane, but they were feeling a bit lost. They had no phones to look at, no Facebook, no Instagram, no YouTube, no Snapchat, no Twitter, no TikTok, and no games to speak of.

Selina was watching slyly to see what they would do without having technology at their fingertips. Summo was the first to get up and move, making his way over to the windows to watch the planes take off and land, while Spence was people watching, which was something he enjoyed doing. Leaf, for his part, was wandering around the lounge area and contemplating the day's happenings.

Selina kept a keen eye on all three of them, even though they had gone off in three different directions. She found it quite amusing seeing them without a phone glued to their hands, as their generation had grown up with tech almost since birth.

Eventually, it was time to board the plane. Selina was used to flying around the world all the time, however the lads on the other hand were feeling wary. The three of them were seated together, while Selina was a couple of rows back so she could keep a watchful eye on them. It wasn't long before all three of them had dozed off in their chairs. From Chile to Cuba would be a six-and-a-half hour flight, so in theory, they would get some solid sleep if there was no turbulence. Luckily enough for the boys, there was very little turbulence, and they were only woken up once the voice of the captain rung out asking everyone to put their seatbelts on as they would be landing shortly. The lads stretched their arms as they slowly emerged from their deep slumber.

They hit the tarmac with the familiar screeching of the tyres, and the boys stood up at the same time, intending to walk off the plane. Suddenly, they found themselves piled on top of each other, with arms and legs everywhere, completely blocking the aisle.

Leaf looked down at his shoes, and discovered that his laces were tied up to both of his mates'. Then they looked up, and found Selina standing above them. "Can you three move? You are blocking the aisle," she said sternly, stepping over them with a smirk on her face. Then she turned around and said, "See you three in the baggage area when you've figured out how to get out of that mess."

The three friends untangled their laces and made haste to the baggage area with annoyed looks on their faces, and Leaf stormed straight up to Selina and got right in her grill.

"What the hell was the big idea?" he said, but before he could finish his sentence, Selina had flipped him around, and bent his right arm against his back in a painful position.

She put her lips up to his ear and whispered, "Who was awake out of you three of you to keep watch?"

Leaf didn't answer. He knew she was right.

"I told you the same thing when we were on the way to Chile," said Selina, pushing Leaf away from her, as he grabbed his arm and gave it a rub.

Then something really odd happened that he didn't expect, when both Spence and Summo charged at Selina. Leaf watched on as what transpired in front of him suddenly seemed to happen in slow motion.

Selina swept Spence's legs out from underneath him, sending him sprawling on to the airport floor, and as quick as a flash she had Summo in a headlock. All of sudden, airport security were running over towards them, as Selina let go of Summo and burst out laughing.

She shot Leaf a wink and he started laughing as well. This must have been some sort of ploy to get out of the situation, thought Leaf, as one guard approached Selina cautiously and spoke to her quickly in Spanish.

Selina responded in Spanish with a few laughs in between, and the five guards all burst out laughing as she finished speaking.

The guards slowly walked away, still laughing, as one guard walked past Leaf and said something in Spanish.

"What did you say?" asked Leaf sheepishly.

"I said that I kick my three brothers' arses all day long. They try to beat me but it has never happened to date," she explained.

"Oh," said Leaf.

As the last guard moved out of eyesight, Selina barked, "Better luck next time! Now get your bags and then park your arses on that bench!"

She stood in front of them like she was the disappointed principal and they were the naughty students. "Did you prefer to die or simply get arrested?" she scolded them.

"What do you mean?" questioned Summo.

"You were all asleep on the plane and you have someone that is tracking you down. Just think about it. Not only that, but you have the sheer stupidity to attack me in a foreign airport," she continued, before storming off towards the exit muttering underneath her breath, "What am I doing dealing with these immature delinquents? I should have asked for more cash for this job."

The lads just sat there on the bench in silence, until eventually, Leaf spoke up. "What the hell where you two thinking attacking Selina like that?"

"We made a promise to Frank to make sure you are kept safe," explained Spence.

Leaf was taken aback by this comment, and his demeanour changed from annoyed to grateful, as he gave both of them a big smile. And when Leaf smiled, you could see all of his teeth, and it looked like his entire face smiled too.

EIGHT

The mates eventually made their way to the exit and met up with Selina outside. They could feel the temperature was a lot warmer than it was in Chile, as their eyes wandered over the unfamiliar landscape before them. There was stunning Spanish architecture all around them, with a huge amount of beautiful brickwork, and the sidewalk and parts of the road were made of pavements woven in unique patterns.

Suddenly, Summo screamed, "Are you guys seeing all this?!"

"Yeah, of course, mate," responded Spence.

"No, no… I mean look at the cars that are driving around. Aren't they the sexiest things you have ever seen?"

Selina leaned over to leaf and asked, "Is he, okay?"

Leaf smiled. "He has a massive thing for cars," he replied.

"Look, there is an old Chevrolet!" shrieked Summo as a pristine red Chevy drove past. "Oh, and look, a Pontiac, a Dodge, and a Buick," he added, pointing at the cars like a little kid in a toy store.

"Why are the cars all old-school here?" questioned Leaf.

"Due to the US trade embargo when Fidel Castro seized power in his revolution," explained Spence.

The three others stared at him in amazement.

"What, you expect me to come to a foreign country and not do detailed research into it?" stated Spence.

"Well, this history lesson is very nice and all, but we need to get out of sight and make our way to where we are staying," said Selina.

"I wish I had my phone so I could take photos of all these cars. It would look so good on my Facebook page. I could show them to my old man as well," declared Summo.

"Well, you don't," said Spence.

"No, but your mate Leaf still does," said Selina, staring at Leaf.

"What, you still have your phone? I thought you binned it in Chile," said Summo.

"I did, but I still have the phone that Frank gave me," explained Leaf, feeling rather nervous.

"Why do you have that phone when he's dead?" asked Summo.

"He kept it because Frank is still alive," answered Spence.

"So, you both knew as well and nobody bothered to tell me," said Summo, who was both annoyed and shocked that his mates had kept him out of the loop.

"He contacted me a bit after his death and made me swear not tell anyone," explained Leaf.

"Spence knew," shot back Summo.

"I was on the phone to Frank and he overheard. I had to tell him mate, come on. You can see where I am coming from," said Leaf.

"Yeah, I can pick up what you're pointing out," said Summo, still in a mood.

"Well, more to the point now is you have a bloody phone that could be tracked," said Selina, who was not happy at all.

"Ah, yeah… well," mumbled Leaf.

"It's a good thing I checked what was in you guys' pockets," followed up Selina.

"I am paying you to keep us safe. That means I am in charge," said Leaf with authority in his voice. His two mates looked at him sideways, as they weren't used to seeing him acting in this manner.

"Yeah, you pay me and I keep you safe," fired back Selina. "But it doesn't mean you're in charge. And you can keep your phone anyway."

"Why is that?" asked Leaf.

"I made changes to it so you can use it without being found," answered Selina.

"How can you do that?" questioned Spence.

"There are lots of things you can do with phones that you have never heard of," explained Selina.

"What do you mean?" followed up Spence.

"It's too hard to explain now, but just don't believe everything you see on TV, or what the government tells you is true," answered Selina.

A mint hot, pink Studebaker pulled up to the curb, and it looked like Summo was going to die of pure enjoyment.

"Leaf, you have to take a photo of me with this car!" shrieked Summo, sounding like a teenybopper at a Justin Bieber concert.

Leaf took out his phone and took several photos of Summo posing in and out of the car. The driver was a middle-aged man with a sharp dress taste, a smart pair of black sunnies, and a light blue dress t-shirt. He was enjoying Summo giving attention to his car, which was clearly his pride and joy going by the immaculate condition he kept it in.

He asked where they would like to go, and his English was more fluid than their driver in Chile.

"I call shot gun!" said Summo, quickly darting to the front seat before anyone else had a chance to even think about it.

The other three hopped in the back of the car, as Selina handed the driver a piece of paper, and he read it and responded, "Yes, *senorita*."

"What was on the paper?" queried Leaf.

"The address of where we are going," said Selina.

Summo turned from the front seat and exclaimed, "This may just be the best day of my life," with a massive grin on his face. "I wish my dad could be here to see all these cars and ride in this beautiful one," he continued.

"Why is he so excited about these cars?" Selina asked Leaf.

"Summo grew up around cars. His old man is a mechanic and owns a couple of classic cars himself, hence him starting a cadetship as a car salesman," answered Leaf.

They made their way through the picturesque city, with its original brick buildings. Some were painted in bright colours that they had never seen before, like a beautiful baby blue, which you would never find on a house back home.

After travelling for a while, the Studebaker stopped in front of a light brown brick building.

"We are here, *senorita*," announced the driver.

They got out of the car, and Selina pulled a key out of her pocket and unlocked the old-looking wooden door to the house.

The three mates followed her in, and as their eyes adjusted to light in the room, they could see old wooden furniture, and an older looking couch, with stairs to their left.

"Make your way upstairs. There are some rooms for each of you, so you can settle in," said Selina.

"What about you?" asked Spence.

"I will sleep on the couch," answered Selina.

"Really?" chimed in Summo in a surprised voice.

"Yes, really," said Selina, "unless you have some sort of martial arts skills you are hiding."

Summo looked backed at her with a blank expression on his face.

"So that's a 'no' then," she said, adding, "this is the only entry point to the building, which means I am the only person that can stop someone else from trying to get in."

The three lads nodded their heads in acknowledgment and headed up the stairs to check out their rooms.

NINE

Leaf made himself comfortable in his small room. It had a single bed, a closet in the other corner, and nothing else, not even a lamp.

He unpacked his suitcase, putting his things into the cupboard, and he came across the book. He sighed deeply as he looked at the cover, with his fingers running over the spine.

He hadn't fully read the part about the population of Xonarye yet, and he still felt nauseous thinking about it. He flipped over the pages with his fingers, trying to decide if it was the right time to read it or not, then he put the book on the bed and made his way back downstairs.

Selina was sitting on the couch scrolling her phone, and she looked up at him as he arrived.

"I was wondering when you would come down," she said.

"Why is that?" asked Leaf.

"Well, we need money to buy supplies, so we need to change some cash," explained Selina. She stood up off the couch and added, "Give me a hand to move this couch away from the wall."

They both grabbed one end of the two-seater couch and slid it away from the wall. Underneath, there was a dusty brown rug that had been through the wars. Selina rolled it up and it revealed a wooden panel in the floor. She jimmied open one end of the wooden panel to find a deep hole dug into the building's foundations.

"What is this hole, and what is this place?" questioned Leaf.

"It's one of the many safe houses I have scattered across the globe, and this hole has supplies of cash, weapons, and other important items," explained Selina. "You need to transfer me some money so I can change it into local currency," she added.

Leaf pulled out his phone and sent the money across into Selina's account, as Selina jumped into the hole and started passing up a couple of bundles of cash. Leaf placed the money on the wooden table, as Selina grabbed a gun with some ammo before climbing back out again.

Selina and Leaf were putting the couch back in place just as Spence and Summo came bounding down the stairs. Their eyes spied the couple of bundles of cash on the table, and the two mates could hardly believe what they were seeing. It was like a scene from a movie.

"Wow, that's a fair bit of cash," said Summo.

"Well, technically, in Cuba the currency is called the Cuban Peso," explained Spence.

Summo shook his head at Spence. "It's cash, money, dollars, bills, bucks, cheddar, clams, greenbacks, gwop, moola, scratch; it all means money, and we can buy so many things with it."

"Are you two finished squabbling like an old married couple?" interjected Selina.

"So, what's the plan to get food Selina?" asked Leaf.

"There is a small market a couple of streets away. We will all make our way down there to buy it," responded Selina.

"Well, let's get organised and make a move down to the market," declared Leaf.

They got themselves ready and made their way towards the market. The street they were walking down was lined with two- and three-story houses that were stacked each side of the road, with big archways as entries, and black rails around the outside of the balconies. The buildings were so different to what the three mates were used to seeing back home.

After about ten minutes or so of walking, they arrived at the small market, and Selina stopped, turned around in front of the three boys and spoke. "We need to all stay together here. I don't want one of you wandering off. I have a reputation to protect."

It was then that Leaf noticed that Selina wasn't wearing her usual leather jacket. Instead, she had on a blue singlet with shorts and a pair of thongs. As she turned back around to walk into the market, something on Selina's left inner bicep caught Leaf's eye.

He thought it was a tattoo of some kind, and he was quite curious about it and needed to find out more.

As they walked through the market, they saw a wide array of things ranging from paintings, to wood handicraft, to coconuts, and from Cuban licence plates, to books, to Cuban flags, Cuban shirts and jewellery. There was rice, fish, chicken, mangos, papayas, avocados, garlic, and beef. You name it, it was there.

There was also the sound of beautiful energetic music that made your body want to groove to the sounds. It came across as a fusion of Jazz and salsa. The locals were talking to them in Spanish, and offering them lots of native foods to try that the three friends had never seen before.

Summo was offered a kind of pink fleshy fruit, and he slowly took a bite out of it. "Oh, my God guys, you need to try this!" he yelled out.

He handed a piece of the unknown fruit to his two mates to try, and they found it delicious.

"We need to buy some of these," announced Summo, "but what are they exactly?"

Selina spoke to the stall owner in Spanish, then she said, "The fruit is called mamey."

They ended up buying some mamey and other food so they could make a meal together that night.

Walking back, everyone seemed happy with their experience at the market. Selina was trotting next to Leaf, and she said, "I think we should have a talk when we get back. I need to know what I am doing here, and why you guys are here as well."

Leaf took a deep gulp and slowly nodded. He was still unsure if he could fully trust her, but he was arriving at a point where he might not have a choice.

Summo sped up a little to catch up with Leaf, and raising his arm in the air, he said, "Have a look at this bracelet I bought." It was a beautiful thinly hand-crafted leather band. "I am so glad I came mate; I can't believe the food I have seen. Things I've never tasted before. And that's without even mentioning the cars," he said with a grin that would rival a kid at Disneyland.

"How you are doing there, Spence?" asked Leaf.

"I might have to pinch myself," said Spence, shaking his head in disbelief. "What about you mate?" he asked.

"Well, so far I am enjoying myself, but tomorrow we need to get down to why we are here."

The mood within the group changed instantly as Leaf finished his sentence.

Once they got back to the house, Spence made his way to the kitchen to prepare something to eat. He knew how to cook, but in his own mind he thought he was the next Master Chef.

Summo made his way upstairs to have a shower and calm down a bit, as he was still so excited about what he had experienced over the past couple of days.

Leaf and Selina were left on their own downstairs to finish their conversation from earlier. "Are you going to answer my question now?" asked Selina.

"I will," said Leaf. "But you need to answer my question first."

Selina raised her eyebrows at him and responded, "Come on then."

"The tattoo on your arm… what is it?" asked Leaf.

She raised her arm, and in black ink it clearly read Kosove, with two dots on top of the 'e.'

"It means Kosovo in Albanian," explained Selina. "Albanian is the primary language in Kosovo."

TEN

"Your home country clearly means a lot to you," said Leaf.

"It's where I am from. My heritage means the world to me," said Selina. "And one day, I hope the entire world will acknowledge Kosovo as a country, not just a province."

Leaf smiled back at Selina. He could feel the love and emotion in her voice as she spoke about Kosovo, however she quickly changed her voice back to her normal tone, as she said, "Now it's your turn to answer my question."

Where do I even start? Leaf thought to himself.

"Well, we are here to find the relative of a person called Nila Runika, who we hope has an item that we require," explained Leaf.

"This item, what is it?" questioned Selina. "It's a belt buckle; the same one as I have been wearing these past few days," answered Leaf.

"You're here for a belt buckle?" snorted Selina. "I am here just to help you find a belt buckle." She was not impressed.

"It's not just any belt buckle," explained Leaf. "It is one of twenty-six in total, and they are very valuable."

"Is that why that lady at the airport was after you?" asked Selina.

"Yes," said Leaf. "She works for a group who are desperate to have all twenty-six of them. She is a dangerous person."

"How is she dangerous exactly?" asked Selina.

"I know a person who has died because of her," answered Leaf.

You could tell Selina was taking it all in and trying to put all the pieces of the puzzle together by the look on her face.

"So, what makes you three so special to find these valuable belt buckles?" asked Selina.

"Well, to be perfectly honest, nothing. I found the belt buckle, and the other guys are my two best mates."

"Let me get this right: you three have no combat skills, or any worldly skills to speak of, and you are going to find all these buckles with a dangerous woman on your tail?" said Selina in dismay.

Leaf just sat there. He wanted to speak but nothing was coming out of his mouth.

"No wonder they hired me to protect you," said Selina. "You three have no idea what you have gotten yourselves into."

Leaf still just sat there in a state of bafflement. It was quite surreal and eye-opening to hear Selina talking so bluntly.

Selina exhaled loudly. "At least tell me more about yourself and the other two."

"Why?" asked Leaf.

"So, I know what you are all capable of," responded Selina.

"Well, I am nineteen, and I was an apprentice builder. Um… Mum is a nurse; Dad a truck driver. Only child, first trip out of the country, and I have no combat skills," said Leaf.

"What about Spence?" questioned Selina.

"Well…" said a voice through the kitchen doorway; it was Spence. "I am also nineteen, and I work on the family farm with my old man. It's a fourth-generation farm. My mum stays at home. I have a sister five years older than me; she lives in Adelaide as a physio. I have been to New Zealand to work and have no combat skills."

"Thank you, 'voice from the kitchen,'!" yelled Selina. "Now the last of the group?" she continued.

Summo appeared around the bottom of the stairwell; he had been there for a little while, eaves dropping on the conversation.

"Hi, my name is Dean Summers. People call me Summo. I am nineteen, and this is my first AA meeting," he said with a laugh.

Leaf let out a bit of a laugh, but Selina sat there stone faced and unimpressed.

"I love cars and was doing a cadetship at a car dealership. My dad is a mechanic, which is where my love of cars comes from. No brothers or sisters. I have been overseas to Tasmania and have secretly trained with ninjas," he said with a laugh at the end as he struck a ninja-like pose.

"What about your mum?" questioned Selina. It had not gone past her that he had said nothing about his mum. Summo's jovial mood quickly changed to sombre, and Selina looked at him, then at Spence, and finally, at Leaf. All three mates had a glum look on each of their faces.

"You don't need to say anything," said Spence.

"Yeah, I know," replied Summo in a meek voice. "My beautiful mum passed away about a year ago from a six-month fight with breast cancer," said Summo, who was getting quite emotional, as a couple of tears trickled down his cheek.

"She was an accountant, loved by everyone she met, and I miss her every day," he continued.

Both Spence and Leaf came over and gave him a hug each.

"What was her name?" asked Selina in a voice that was showing just a little more empathy than before.

Summo smiled. "Her name was Bonnie."

Selina smiled back at him. "That's a beautiful name."

"Now I know what I am doing here, why you're here, and what your capabilities are. That helps me a lot," explained Selina. "And one thing I know about you already, which will be very important moving forward, is that you have each other's backs," she added.

The three mates gave each other a small smile.

"Spence, is dinner getting close to being ready?" asked Selina.

"Yeah, grub will be up shortly," replied Spence.

Shortly after, they all sat down to eat the food Spence had prepared for them. It was some sort of tasty chicken broth would be the best way to describe it. During that time, Selina went to the top shelf of a cupboard and came back with some Cuban rum, which she poured into glasses for everyone.

Then, she picked up her glass and raised it to family, with the three mates clinking glasses with her and saying "to family" as well.

"So, Selina," said Leaf, "we already heard a little about you, how about you tell us a bit more?"

"You know enough," she replied sharply.

"Come on, it can't hurt," piped up Summo.

"It's not a good Idea, I have been in this business long enough," said Selina.

"How about just one question?" said Spence, trying to think more logically about it.

"Oh, okay," said Selina, who was beginning to get annoyed by the situation.

"How old are you?" blurted out Summo before anyone else had time to stop him.

"Really, mate?" groaned Leaf with his hands on his head.

"You can't ask a woman that," said Spence. "It's extremely bad manners."

"Well, if that's your question," said Selina, "I am thirty-five."

Spence gave his mates a big toothy smile, and they just shook their heads back at him in disbelief.

They finished up eating their food, which had filled a nice hole in all of their bellies, and they were sitting in the lounge having a drink of rum, when Summo suddenly jumped off the couch and headed into the kitchen.

"What's he up to?" asked Spence.

"Who would know?" replied Leaf with a shrug of his shoulders.

A few minutes later, Summo came back in looking very proud of himself. He was carrying a platter of mamey that he had cut into pieces to share with everyone.

"This has to be one of the nicest things I have tried," proclaimed Summo.

"It's not bad, I must admit," said Selina. "But just wait till you get to some other countries and experience the whole host of delicacies out there waiting to be discovered."

ELEVEN

After they finished eating the mamey, Selina did something that surprised the other three in the room, when she pulled a smoke out of her pocket and lit it up.

She looked at the other three, who were staring a hole through her.

"What?" she said with a deadpan look on her face.

"Well, I don't think that any of us picked you as a smoker," explained Spence.

"Like I said, the less you know the better," responded Selina.

"Haven't you guys tried smoking before?" she followed on.

"We all tried it a couple of years ago. It felt like I was going to cough up a lung," said Summo, who looked like he was experiencing it all over again.

"Each to their own," said Selina.

"You know that it's bad for your health?" chimed in Leaf, and Selina looked at him and said, "A lot of things are bad for you. I am not forcing you to smoke now, am I?"

"Well, um… no," answered Leaf quietly.

"Then I am not hurting any of you," she said as she let out a puff of smoke through her nostrils.

Much to everyone's surprise, Summo said, "You know what I wouldn't mind trying is a Cuban cigar. You see people in movies smoking them and it looks cool."

Spence and Leaf turned their heads on an angle and looked at him quite puzzled.

"Well, I have cigars here hidden away. You can try one if you like?" said Selina.

You could see the wheels spinning around in Summo's head, before he said, "Why not? May as well try a fresh experience while I'm here."

Selina looked at the other two and said, "Would you like to try too? It's only a question; I am not forcing you."

Spence, who was the thinker of the three mates, said, "Why not? It makes sense to me to try a fresh experience while I'm in a foreign country."

That just left Leaf with a decision to make, as the other three gazed at him, waiting for his response. "I am all for trying new things, but this doesn't interest me one little bit," said Leaf.

"Okay, three cigars it is," said Selina, getting up and strolling into the kitchen. She came back holding a small brown wooden box in her right hand. Placing it on the coffee table, she opened the lid to reveal a range of cigars, a bright silver lighter, and a black cigar cutter.

Selina looked at the different cigars in the box and selected three, handing one each to Summo and Spence.

"Why are these different to yours Selina?" questioned Leaf.

"There are different strengths, and I don't think they will be able take the taste of mine compared to the ones I have selected them for them," explained Selina, picking up the cigar cutter, and showing the other two how to cut the cigar.

She cut the end of her cigar and passed it to Summo and Spence to do the same. Then, picking up the silver lighter, she slowly lit the other end up while taking small puffs to get it glowing. She passed the lighter over to Summo, who slowly started to light up his cigar.

"Now, don't inhale the smoke into to your lungs," cautioned Selina.

Summo got a good glow on the end of his cigar and gradually started to puff away on it, then Spence took the lighter and was about to light the end up when Summo made a little cough.

"Must have taken a bit of smoke down," he said with a cheeky smile. Spence lit his end of the cigar up and slowly puffed away as well, while

Leaf just sat there watching the three of them puff away, the red glow at the end of the cigars and the smoke starting to fill the room.

Leaf had a last sip of his rum and said "goodnight," leaving the three to finish their cigars. It definitely wasn't his cup of tea.

Shortly after, Leaf lay there on his bed that was surprisingly comfy for a small baren room. He laid this way and that, trying to get to sleep, but he could not seem to manage.

He heard footsteps coming up the stairs and figured it must be Spence and Summo after finally finishing up for the evening.

Eventually, he got up and walked over to his backpack to get his phone and see what the time was. When he unlocked his phone, the screen light shone directly into the bag, and the book that had started this unexpected journey caught his eye.

He picked it up, wandered back over to the bed, and sat down. Then he sat there with the book in one hand and the phone Frank gave him in the other, just contemplating the items. His thoughts kept going back to the only chapter he hadn't been able to read yet.

He flicked through the pages with his fingers until he came to the section about the population, then he took a big deep breath, sighing loudly and trying to sike himself up, as if he were finding courage before going to battle.

If I can't even read this, how am I going to cope with harder things that come my way on this journey? he thought. *It's time to do this.* His eyes adjusted to the light of the phone as they started wandering over the words on the page.

The population of our magnificent country was spread far and wide, from the twin cities to vast areas of the smaller towns. The total population was 17.5 million strong. The noble capital, Langeth had the largest population, with 3.5 million people dwelling there. The other twin city, Fasmara had a population of 3 million. The other 5 great cities made up the majority of the population. Wex Wex with 2.2 million, Cintama with 1.9 million, Dahn with 1.4 million, Spintex with 1.2 million, and finally Mintogh with 1.2 million. That left approximately 2.3 million people scattered across this magnificent country of ours. 17.5 million strong beautiful people called this magnificent proud country Xonarye home.

Leaf sat there on the bed in silence trying to wrap his head around what he had just read. Out of seventeen and a half million people, only twenty-six were able to survive and escape from the terrible virus.

"Only twenty-six survived," Leaf said to himself. He felt coldness deep within his soul saying it out loud. His stomach started to churn painfully, as other questions popped into his mind.

How could he and his mates pull this off? Also, how in the hell did Summo and Spence read this and not say anything to him? Or maybe they hadn't been able to bring themselves to read this chapter either. He would have to try and get some sleep and look for answers in the morning.

TWELVE

Leaf woke up in the morning feeling like he hadn't slept for at least two days. God only knew what he actually looked like.

He trudged slowly down the hallway then made his way down the creaky staircase. Spence and Summo were downstairs drinking a cup of coffee each in the lounge area looking fresh as daisy.

"Whoa mate, what happened to you?" exclaimed Summo.

"I have a better question for you two," snapped Leaf, clearly heavily sleep deprived. "Have either of you read the chapter of the book about the population of Xonarye?"

Spence and Summo looked at each other, then back at Leaf, both tentatively shaking their heads.

Leaf's mood improved as he realised, they hadn't kept it from him. "Why not?" he asked in a nicer tone.

"Are you joking? I didn't want to know how many people had passed away," said Spence.

"Me neither mate," chimed in Summo.

Leaf let out a loud, "Oh."

"Hang on mate, you actually read it?" asked Spence disbelievingly. Leaf nodded his heavy head with a weight wrapped around his heart.

"How did you manage to do that?" questioned Summo.

"I had to. If I couldn't read that, how could I deal with the harder situations that we might have to face?" replied Leaf.

His two mates just stared at him in disbelief.

"Come on guys, let's face it, it will not always be beers and skittles like the last couple of days," said Leaf.

"He's right, you know," came a voice from behind them. It was Selina, making her way down the creaky stairs without them hearing her.

"Where did you come from?" asked Leaf in surprise.

"I am allowed to have a shower, you know? I don't need your permission," she teased.

"So, are you going to tell me about this chapter of a book you read?" questioned Selina.

Leaf stood there for a minute thinking that if he told her this much, then everything would have to come out.

"Preferably, while we are still young," snapped Selina.

"The part of the book I read was about the population of Xonarye," said Leaf. "It was seventeen and a half million people."

"You're bloody joking, mate, aren't you?" said Spence.

"I really wish I was," said Leaf in a sombre voice.

Selina sat there watching the lads' reactions to what Leaf had just said. She didn't know what he was going on about, but it was clearly important. Suddenly, she grabbed Leaf by the shoulders and spun him around to face her.

"Tell me the rest of the story about why the hell you are here!" she yelled.

"The belt buckles open a door… a door to a country called Xonarye that has been lost undersea for a bloody long time. The population was seventeen and a half million, but only twenty-six people escaped a deadly virus," said Leaf in a quick loud manner without taking a breath.

Selina just looked at him and then at the other two like they were taking the piss out of her. Then, as quick as wink, she grabbed Leaf's arm and twisted it around his back.

"Will someone tell me the truth before I snap his arm off!" she shouted.

"It's true," said Summo.

Selina raised her left eyebrow frighteningly.

"Get the book!" said Leaf, "before she breaks my arm."

Summo took off up the stairs to grab the book out of Leaf's room.

Then, running back down the stairs, he tossed it to Selina, who snatched it out of the air and let go of Leaf's arm while pushing him to the floor.

She examined the outside of the book and looked at them. "So this is what all the fuss is about."

"Yes, it is," answered Spence. "Just read it."

"That's a great idea," said Leaf, picking himself up off the floor and rubbing his shoulder.

"You can read the book. I am going to have a shower, and then we can get on with finding the relative of Nila Runika," continued an annoyed Leaf.

The shower was what Leaf needed after his restless night and getting his shoulder almost twisted off his body. Making his way back downstairs, he found Selina sitting in the armchair waving the book in her right hand. There was no sign of Spence or Summo.

"How was the book? I hope it has sorted everything out," stated Leaf.

"Well, it is very interesting," responded Selina in a sarcastic voice.

Leaf was almost expecting her to think it was some half-arsed fairytale, so he handed her the paperwork that he had signed to get the money out of the bank. She read it and shrugged her shoulders.

Then he took the coins he had found in the book's spine and handed them to Selina. Again, she had a look and shrugged her shoulders. Leaf was getting annoyed at her now, so he undid his belt and handed it to Selina, allowing her to study the buckle.

Again, she looked, and then shrugged her shoulders in disbelief. "Are you frigging serious?" yelled Leaf in frustration.

"What, nothing else to show me?" said Selina mockingly.

"No" said a defeated Leaf.

"Well, now I know everything," said Selina with a smile as she handed the things back to Leaf.

"What, you believe me?" said Leaf in a confused voice.

"Yes," said Selina. "I just wanted to make sure I know everything so there are no more unexpected surprises."

"You played me," said Leaf, feeling deflated.

"Hmm… yup, I did, just like a fiddle. You better not let things slip so easily in the future," said Selina in a teasing manner.

Spence and Summo came bounding down the stairs together.

"So, we all sweet?" asked Summo.

"Yeah, everything is just peachy," said Leaf in a childish voice.

Spence looked at him with raised eyebrows and mouthed '*what?*'

"Don't worry about him," said Selina. "I got him to tell me basically everything without even really trying."

"Everything. Really?" said Summo.

"Yes, really," said Leaf, who was feeling rather steamed off about the situation.

"Look, don't worry about it. I am trained to get info out of people. Have a look on the bright side, I didn't have to torture you," said Selina.

"Torture," repeated Summo, laughing loudly.

Selina leered at Summo. "You saw how quickly I twisted his arm and you went running for the book. I could have done a lot more."

Summo didn't see it as a laughing matter anymore.

"So, the plan is to find the relative of this Nila Runika?" said Selina, changing her voice back to her normal tone.

"Yes, that's the plan," repeated Leaf. "There is a Café in the middle of Havana called Café el Runika. Hopefully, it will lead us to the next belt buckle, and a clue for the following one as well," he explained.

"Really, that's the plan? Well, it's your money," said Selina, clearly unimpressed with what Leaf had in mind.

THIRTEEN

Selina started dialling numbers on her phone, then she spoke to someone in Spanish. Once she was finished, she proclaimed, "A car will be here in five minutes to take us to the café."

The mates made their way back to their rooms to chuck some new clothes on for the day, and when they walked out of the front door, it was a beautiful summer's day outside.

Suddenly, Summo let out a shriek.

"What is it?" asked Spence, looking quite puzzled at his mate.

"Have you seen that amazing car in front of us?" he exclaimed.

"Yeah mate, we did, but how about you tell us what we are looking at?" said Leaf with a smile. Spence just smiled back at Leaf, both of them clearly happy to see their mate in his element.

"What your eyes are feasting on right this very moment is a Star Chief Pontiac in a beautiful cherry red, with a crisp white collapsible roof," explained Summo. "It was made between 1954 and 1966, and from memory it should have a 4-cylinder motor, just to name a few features," continued Summo.

Then, turning to Selina, he said, "I could just hug you," and he advanced towards her to do just that, before she grabbed him and twisted his arm around his back, bending him over the boot of the car.

"I don't do hugs; especially with people I am paid to protect."

"Come on Summo, stop stuffing around and get in the car," said

Leaf, as Selina released Summo's arm and he yelled "shotgun" and climbed into the front seat of the cherry red car.

They were cruising along in a stunning car, with the warm sun on their skin, and the wind wafting through their hair in this gorgeous foreign country.

"Now this is living!" Summo shouted from the front seat.

Suddenly, the car came to a grinding halt and Summo just managed to get a hand on the dash to keep his skull from giving it an all-mighty whack. There had been a car accident in front of them, and the driver had done well not to add to the pile of carnage. They had to make a detour down a side road, and they didn't make it far that way either, as there was a stack of wooden crates blocking their path.

The driver and the three mates looked puzzled at the situation in front of them. Selina, however, had pulled out a small hand gun from behind her back and was holding it at the ready. The three mates did not know where she had whipped it out from, or even that she way carrying a gun on her.

She turned to the driver and said, "Get us out of here, now!" The driver chucked it into reverse at great speed, and as they sped along backwards a figure appeared from behind the wooden crates.

"That's her!" yelled Leaf. "That's Tamina Suva!" He stood up in the back of the car and pointed at her. The other two mates' jaws dropped just like characters from a kids' cartoon, as the driver swung the car around the corner and switched into first gear.

"Take us back to where you picked us up!" demanded Selina, turning around and eye-bawling each of the three mates in the back seat.

After a while, the car came to a grinding stop outside the front door of their hideout.

"Grab you gear from inside and get your backsides back in the car in two minutes or you get left behind!" bellowed Selina. The boys scrambled out of the car and clambered up the creaky stairs to grab their bags. Then, before they even had a chance to sit back down in the car, it was speeding off again.

They zipped in and out of the streets in a crazy random pattern, with the three boys looking completely puzzled by the whole situation.

"What's going on?" whispered Summo to Leaf and Spence. They

both shrugged their shoulders in response to their mate's question and just sat in the back seat in silence. Selina had not said a word or looked at them since they had left her safe house. Their surroundings were changing from rows of buildings to more spread-out ones interspersed with trees. They were heading out of Havana, but they did not know why, where, or in which direction they were heading.

After another twenty minutes of driving out into the countryside, the car went down a couple of dirt roads and pulled up under the shade of a tree.

"Everyone out of the car!" commanded Selina. She was clearly not happy about what had transpired earlier on the way to the café. She was pacing back and forth in front of them, stopping now and then to stare at each of them in turn.

"I know none of you would turn on each other, so I need to know who else knows about this journey," she barked.

"Um… well, it's just us and Frank," said Leaf. "And it can't be Frank, because we are paying him just like we are paying you."

"Are you sure no one else knows?" said Selina, looking very suspiciously at them.

"No one else," replied Spence.

Her eyes wandered over to Summo, who quickly shook his head vigorously back at her.

Selina continued pacing again, trying to figure out what had just happened.

"How did she find us?" asked Leaf.

"That's what I am trying to figure out," said Selina gruffly. "Who else has seen the book you are carrying?" she added.

"Only us and Frank," responded Spence.

"What else have you had on you since you left?" said Selina.

"Our clothes?" said Summo looking clueless.

"We got rid of our phones," added Spence.

"You checked the phone Frank gave me," said Leaf.

Selina didn't answer and kept pacing around on the dirt road.

"The paperwork you took to the bank. You still have it on you, don't you Leaf?" said Selina suddenly.

Leaf pulled the papers out of his bag and handed them to Selina with a confused look on his face. Then Selina carefully studied the front side, then she spun them around and looked at the back. Suddenly, she pulled out her lighter and lit the papers on fire.

"What are you doing?" shouted Spence, looking bewildered.

Selina just put her finger up to her lips to shush him, laid the burning papers on the ground, and observed the fire attentively.

The other three gathered around and joined her, though they clearly did not know what was going judging by the look on their faces. Eventually, the papers disappeared in a pile of ashes on the ground, and Selina started sifting through until she came out with something very tiny on the little finger of her right hand.

FOURTEEN

The other three were trying to work out what she was staring at on her little finger.

"This is how the hell they found us!" shouted Selina, waving her little finger under their noses. She squished whatever it was between her little finger and her thumb, and she grabbed her mobile phone and walked away in the opposite direction looking highly animated.

"What just happened?" asked Summo.

Spence and Leaf looked back blankly at him; they had no clue either.

After a moment, Selina stormed back over. "Do you know what you have done?" she said, glaring at them.

Spence and Summo just stood there like stone, unable to move or speak.

"How about you tell us what the heck is going on and why you have a bee in your bonnet!" barked Leaf.

His mates were shocked to see him standing up to her. It was highly unusual behaviour for him. Selina's eyes locked onto Leaf's, as they entered into a kind of Mexican standoff.

"Tell us, Selina. What is going on?" asked Leaf in a much calmer tone again.

With the change in tone, Selina's demeanour also changed. "You were being tracked by the thing I squashed, and now I have had to pay someone a large amount of money to clear out my safe house here. That's why there is a bee in my bonnet," explained Selina.

"Thank you," said Leaf. "Now at least we have some idea of what is going on at last."

"Let me get this straight," said Spence. "If he was being tracked, shouldn't we be getting out of here?"

"Yeah, I agree with Spence. We need to put the pedal to the metal," said Summo.

"Yeah, but where are we going to go?" questioned Leaf. "We need a plan, Selina."

Selina looked at him in surprise.

"This is your world and we need your expertise," clarified Leaf.

Selina nodded her head in approval. "Right, get all of your arses back in the car," she demanded, and the boys filed into the back seat and buckled in. Selina then spoke to the driver in Spanish, who seemed unfazed about the situation he had found himself in.

Leaf leaned forward to talk to Selina. "So, where are we going?"

"We are going to skirt around the city and head west to Mariel. It should take us about half an hour to get there," explained Selina, as the boys just sat back and took in the views, while also trying to piece together what had happen.

As they were driving along, Spence finally spoke up. "There are only two people who could have put that tracking device on the paperwork."

"I know," said Leaf in grievance.

"Who?" asked Summo with a puzzled look on his face.

"Either Wilford at the bank, or Frank," explained Spence.

"Well, there are other options, I suppose," said Summo.

His two mates looked at him sideways.

"The three of us and Selina have also handled it."

Spence put his hands on his face, and Leaf's facial expression just read 'wtf?'

Selina was unmoved by the stupidness of Summo's latest statement.

"Tell me in any way shape or form, why one of us or Selina would track ourselves?" asked Spence.

"No, I didn't mean that, but you just said it could only be Wilford or Frank."

"Can you put a filter in your brain before you open your mouth?" said Spence, who was clearly frustrated with his mate.

Leaf started laughing at them both. He needed a good laugh to let off a bit of the tension from this morning's events.

They finally started coming into a town that they had been catching glimpses of every now and then as the sunlight bounced off the water in the Bay of Mariel.

They stopped out the front of a small quaint hotel in Mariel, and they grabbed the gear from the car and made their way inside. Selina spoke to the lady behind the counter about organising a room for all of them to stay there, then once in the room, they dropped the gear on the floor and sat on the ends of their single beds.

"We need to figure out what has happened and where we go next," said Spence thoughtfully.

"Well, as we discussed in the car, there are two people that could have placed the tracker on the papers," said Leaf.

"Well, Wilford is dead, and why would he do it anyway?" asked Summo.

"Is he dead?" said Selina.

"Frank told us he had died," responded Summo sharply.

"You though Frank had died and Frank is the other person who could have placed it there," said Selina.

"Oh," said Summo, his mind clearly trying to keep up.

"What do you think, Selina?" asked Spence.

"My assumption is that it would be the bank manager, Wilford," answered Selina.

"Why?" asked Spence.

"You are paying Frank still, and he contacted you after he faked is death. There is no reason for him to place the tracker on it," explained Selina.

"Wilford told Frank that Tamina visited him to see what he would do. It only makes sense that it was Wilford," continued Selina.

"Then why did he put the tracking device on the paperwork?" asked Leaf.

"There are only two logical reasons: either he was forced to and he is actually dead, or he is a part of Reblick," said Selina.

The lads just sat there for a minute, taking in what Selina had spoken about.

"Why didn't Tamina come to the place where we were staying?" asked Spence.

"That's the thing that I am trying to figure out, because it is bothering me most of all," answered Selina.

"Either way, we are not being tracked anymore, so that's a positive," said Leaf.

"As fair as I am aware," said Selina.

"Good. That means we are safe, and I can go get some fresh air," said Leaf.

Selina looked at him in a weird way.

"Do you have an issue with that, Selina?" asked Leaf.

"No, go for a walk. Just be back in thirty minutes," replied Selina, and Leaf left the room and the others behind. He was looking forward to getting some fresh air and some alone time. He enjoyed being alone sometimes, and fresh air for his head, and being able to stretch his legs after being in the car for most of the day was a great thing for him mentally.

It was also great for him to see the picturesque town of Mariel on this beautiful day.

Leaf arrived back at the hotel room after getting some fresh air, and he found that his two mates had gotten an early night, while Selina was sitting on the bed on her phone.

Leaf thought it was odd that she was on her phone.

"What happened with your safe house?" asked Leaf.

Selina raised her eyebrows in surprise that he had asked that sort of question. "Well, thanks to you three, that place is no longer safe. I had to pay someone to empty the money and the other important items," explained Selina in an annoyed tone.

FIFTEEN

Leaf could tell by the tone in her voice that she was not a happy camper.

"Well, seeing that it was our fault, I will pay for the costs," said Leaf, showing some empathy.

Again, Selina raised her eyebrows at Leaf, as if she were trying to figure out if he was up to something.

"When I get the bill, I will let you know," said Selina, lowering her eyebrows at last.

"Sounds like a solid plan to me," said Leaf with a smile on his face. "What are our next moves going to be?" he asked while lying down on his bed.

"I am trying to work that out," said Selina. "We might lay low for a couple of days then make our way back to Havana."

Leaf kept looking over at Selina, and she didn't seem like herself. It was as if something was still eating away at her.

"What's going on in your head?" he finally asked.

She looked at him and made a twitching motion with her mouth. "Well, if you must know, the first thing is the question that Spence asked earlier today: why didn't she come for us at my safe house?" explained Selina. "Which makes me wonder what type of person we are dealing with."

Leaf sat there listening to Selina while nodding his head in agreement.

"What about the knife she was holding in her hand?" asked Leaf?

Selina half smiled. "Well it looks like someone is being a bit more observant after all," complimented Selina. "To be honest, that doesn't bother me."

"Why not?" asked Leaf.

"Well, everyone needs some sort of weapon or protection in this game, and that is clearly hers," answered Selina.

"What's yours then?" asked Leaf curiously.

"What, you haven't figured that out yet?" she replied in a teasing manner.

"You are looking at my weapon; it's me myself. My hands, arms, legs, head; my entire body has been trained as a living breathing weapon."

Leaf sat there thinking about her answer and remembered how easy she had dealt with them at the airport.

"What have you been trained in?" he asked.

"How about I tell you another day? It's been a big day and we all should get some sleep," suggested Selina.

Leaf was having none of Selina's suggestion however; he wanted to know now. "I am not that tired really Selina, and I am so interested in learning about your training."

Selina looked at him in surprise. He seemed to have a habit of surprising her, which was a hard thing to do at the best of times.

"Well, seeing as you are being persistent about the matter," replied Selina, "I have been trained in the ancient art of Aikido."

The blank look on Leaf's face said it all; he had absolutely no bloody idea what she was talking about.

Selina took a deep breath and decided to educate him on her art. "Aikido is a form of Japanese martial arts which has a couple of meanings depending on who you talk to: unification of your spiritual energy, or the way of harmony."

Leaf was captivated by Selina's every word, as she continued, "The idea is to use the momentum and strength of your opponent against them."

"Do you use lots of strikes and kicks?" quizzed Leaf.

"No, you use a lot of turning motions, pushing movements, and joint locks, just like the one I did with your arm," replied Selina with a smile. "Now you know it's time for you to get some sleep. It's been a long day."

Leaf woke up from a solid night of shut eye, which he clearly needed from all the travelling over the past couple of days.

Summo and Spence where already up and about in the room but Selina was nowhere to be seen.

"Morning sleeping beauty," teased Summo.

"Where's Selina?" asked Leaf in a groggy voice.

"I have no idea," answered Spence.

"Well, that's as handy as a hole in the head," commented Summo.

Just then, Selina walked through the door of the hotel room. She was quite sweaty and wearing exercise clothes.

"Well, well, well… speak of the devil," said Summo.

Selina's gaze fixed on him. "I could be the devil if you want me to be."

"Where have you been?" questioned Spence, breaking up the odd conversation between Summo and Selina.

"Well, if you must know, I went for a run. I need to keep fit and healthy to do my job," answered Selina.

"Then who had our backs while you did that? In case you forgot, we have someone hunting us down," commented Spence.

"You three are safe and have nothing to worry about," answered Selina.

"Why is that?" asked Leaf, who had been sitting quietly, taking in the conversation.

"I have a system," responded Selina.

"Which is?" followed up Leaf.

"I just said you don't need to worry about that. I have it under control. That's why you are paying me," answered Selina.

"Well, that's good enough for me," answered Leaf sternly.

Summo and Spence looked like they would not push the issue, but Leaf looked at them and shook his head nonetheless.

Selina just ignored them all, as Spence went over and sat at the foot of Leaf's bed. "I have been thinking about a couple of things that are bothering me, mate," he said.

"Such as?" asked Leaf.

"The first thing, which we sort of discussed a bit yesterday, is why they didn't come for us at the safe house," said Spence.

"I have been thinking about that too mate, and I think the answer is standing over there," said Leaf, pointing at Selina.

"That's an excellent point," said Spence.

"I have a better question than that though," continued Leaf.

"What would that be mate?" asked Spence.

"Well, the question is for Selina actually."

"Well, there's a surprise," said Selina in a sarcastic tone.

"I can't imagine that there are many people like you and Tamina in this line of work," stated Leaf.

You could see Spence and Summo's faces twig to where Leaf was going.

"I think you know who Tamina is and you haven't bothered to tell the truth," said Leaf, who was finally figuring out when to pick his battles with Selina.

His two mates where now staring at Selina, waiting for her response, as she stood there for a couple of moments in silence with her back to the three of them.

She slowly turned to them and spoke. "You are right, there are few people in this line of work," said Selina. "And I know who Tamina is."

SIXTEEN

"That's just great," groaned Summo out loud, throwing his hands up in the air in disgust.

"Are you kidding me?" complained Spence. "We have been trying to figure out who she is for ages, and you just treated us like we are a bunch of dummies." He couldn't believe Selina's behaviour.

"It's my job to keep you safe and not add stress about her," said Selina, speaking quite gruffly to justify her decision.

"Is this how you would normally operate?" asked Leaf in a calm tone.

"Yes, it is," answered Selina. "It's my job to ensure your safety. That's why you are paying me. None of my other clients ask this many questions and want so many details," she continued.

"Thank you," replied Leaf with a bit of smile of his face.

"Thank you?" blurted out Summo. "How can we trust her now?" He was clearly not happy with the conversation that had just taken place.

"Summo, chill mate. This is what she does for a living," said Leaf, trying to calm him down.

Summo just stood there brooding over the situation.

Spence had been quiet for a bit, thinking about his next words. "Seeing as we are your clients, Selina, don't you think it would be in our best interest to discuss what you know about Tamina for our own safety?" he suggested.

"Oh yeah, that's what I am talking about. Check mate!" yelled out Summo in support.

Spence and Leaf just buried their heads in their hands. Sometimes, there was just no explanation for what went on in their mate's head.

Selina looked at him. "What are you his hype man carrying on that way?" she said. Then, she turned her attention back to Spence. "You make a very interesting and logical argument about the situation we are in," she said, pacing back-and-forth a couple of times, and mulling over the circumstance.

"All right, I will tell you about Tamina," she finally said. "Everyone take a seat around the table."

Once they had sat down, she said, "We used to be friends what seems like a lifetime ago. Tamina was great at protecting people, almost the best in the business. She knew all the protocols inside and out."

"Hang on, she used to protect people for a living?" interrupted Summo.

"Yes, she did," answered Selina.

"What went wrong?" asked Leaf currishly.

"Tamina took a job that I didn't have time to do and I endorsed her for it. Then, the job went pear-shaped, and her client died. She even took a couple of bullets to add further insult to injury," explained Selina.

"Let me guess," said Spence, "she blamed you for the job going wrong."

"Yes, she blamed me for the job going bad and the bullets she received," said Selina.

She stood up from the table, put a smoke in her mouth, lit it up, and took a long drag. You could just tell that this had all had a major impact on her life.

"What happened on the job that went pear-shaped?" asked Leaf.

"Tamina's client was betrayed by someone close to him. Tamina took the first two bullets, but the third took out her client," said Selina. "It hurt her reputation, but more importantly to Tamina, her pride. She followed every protocol to the letter, and I would have taken all the same precautions she did," she continued.

"So, because of this, she flipped to the other side to become an assassin?" asked Leaf.

"As you put it Leaf, she flipped for revenge, and bigger pay days as well," said Selina.

"Is she a good assassin?" quizzed Summo.

Selina puffed out a smoke ring in Summo's direction. "Let me ask you a question, Dean," she said. "You have someone that is highly trained at protecting people, and knows the protocols like the back of her hand. Do you think she would make a good assassin?"

It was odd to hear someone call Summo by his actual name. He would only get called Dean by his mum, or when he was at work. Summo tilted his head sideways. "Well Selina, from what you have said, I think she must be bloody good at what she does."

"I have a better question for you," said Leaf. "Are you better at your Job than Tamina?"

Selina's eyes locked onto Leaf's with immense intensity, like a death stare, but Leaf didn't blink. Instead, he just stared straight back at her.

"That's all I needed to know," commented Leaf, standing up from the table. "Now we have got that all sorted out," he announced, "I think the three of us will follow your lead Selina and get some exercise of our own."

"Aren't you forgetting something?" chimed in Summo.

Leaf looked at his mate with a blank expression.

"Spence had a couple of questions," Summo reminded him.

"Yeah, true that," responded Leaf.

Spence had a very serious expression on his face. "The tracker that was on the paperwork… you took it back to Naracoorte and into your parents' house." You could see the colour slowly drain from Leaf's face as Spence's words rattled around in his head.

The room was in complete silence as all eyes locked on Leaf. He felt coldness and numbness sweep over his body; the same feeling he'd experienced when Red had to let him go from his job.

The thought of something happening to his parents made him feel sick deep in the pit of his stomach. Finally, his brain started to think about a solution rather than the worst-case scenario. "Selina, can you help to keep my parents safe?" he asked in a very shaky voice as he tried to keep it together.

"You know I can help you Leaf. It's just going to cost you, and I must see if the right person is available for both your parents' protection," explained Selina.

Leaf got out his phone and transferred the money over to Selina's bank account, his fingers quite shaky during the entire process.

"Who do you trust with my parents' lives?" asked Leaf anxiously.

Selina cleared her throat. "The first person I was thinking of is already working for me here at the moment," said Selina.

"Excuse me, what do you mean?" piped up Summo.

"I always use my associate to work the perimeter of every job I take. It gives me another set of eyes and an extra layer of protection," explained Selina.

"Do you trust your associate?" asked Spence.

Without hesitation, she responded, "He has saved my life countless times, many of my clients' lives tenfold, and I trust him with my life. And, for your information, you are already trusting him with your life," said Selina with much gusto.

SEVENTEEN

"**W**ho is the associate that you work with?" queried Spence.

"My associate is also my mentor. His name is Ahren, which in German means eagle."

"Eagle," repeated Leaf. "That's very fittings seeing as he is guarding you from afar like a bird of prey."

Selina nodded her head in agreement with Leaf's statement.

"Then if not your mentor, who do you trust that can keep my parents safe from Tamina and Reblick?" asked Leaf.

"How about you three go get some exercise and I will make some enquires on who is available at the moment?" suggested Selina.

"Getting some exercise and fresh air sounds amazing," said Summo enthusiastically, as the three mates got themselves organised for a run.

It was a beautiful morning in Mariel, with the perfect conditionals for running. "Let's run towards the bay?" suggested Leaf, and his two mates smiled in agreement.

Their run was more of a jog, and they all felt good stretching their legs and taking in the new sights down by the beautiful bay, breathing in the fantastic fresh air.

The houses were a lot different to what they had seen in Havana, where there were predominantly two-story buildings stacked together like sardines. Here in Mariel, there was a mixture of two-story and single-story houses, and they were much more spread out. The many archway shapes in Havana had been replaced with square and round pillars out the front of almost every house, holding up solid looking verandas.

The three mates came to a wharf near the edge of the bay, and after they had caught their breath, they gazed out over the beautiful ocean.

"Wow, look over there!" exclaimed Summo, pointing to an area where hundreds of shipping containers were stacked.

"This is a major port for Cuba. Its bay is deeper than the one in Havana, and well placed to deal with many other countries like Jamaica, Panama, the Bahamas, the Dominican Republic, and the United States," exclaimed Spence.

Summo looked at Spence. "Really mate, where did you get this information from?"

Leaf jumped in before Spence had a chance to answer. "Don't you remember he was asked to study Cuba as a research topic? And we all know how much Spence loves information," he said, giving Spence a pat on the back.

There were plenty of locals walking around, and they were having a good gawk at the friends, standing out like sore thumbs compared to everyone else."

"Have you three seen enough?" came a deep rough voice with a thick accent from behind them. Quickly turning around, they had to crane their necks up to see the face on the man mountain that stood in front of them.

The person standing in front of them was a seven foot tall muscle-bound man who appeared to be in his early fifties, with short grey hair, a short, neatly manicured goatee, and you could see part of a sleeve tattoo that stretched up his entire arm.

Leaf looked hard at the tattoo, trying to decipher what he could see before it disappeared up under the man's shirt. It was the shapes, sizes, types, and colours of eagles.

"Going by your accent and the tattoos on your arm, I am going to go out on a limb and say that you must be Ahren, Selina's mentor," presumed Leaf.

Ahren looked down at Leaf. "Hmm, Miss Delacruise made a note that you had become more observant since she first met you, Mr. Brodie."

Summo stood there just staring at Ahren, completely mesmerised by the shear height and size of the man.

"To answer your question, I am not sure we have, unless there is a pressing need for us to head back?" commentated Spence.

Ahren smiled. "Mr. Blake, the logical one of the of the three of you."

"That just leaves Mr. Summers—" Before Ahren could finish, Summo interrupted, "I know what you are going to say: the good looking, charming one of the group."

Ahren looked at him, then at the other two, and then let out a big, booming, almost uncontrollable, laugh.

When his laughter had finally subsided, he said, "I haven't laughed that hard in years. Thank you for that, Mr. Summers."

Summo looked dumbfounded by Ahren's reaction as he had been quite serious.

"Mr Summers, Miss Delacruise finds you funny, and… what's the right word… um… a bit of an airhead," chuckled Ahren.

The second part of the sentence went straight over Summo's head.

"Do you hear? She thinks I am funny," said Summo, elbowing Spence in the ribs with a big smile beaming across his face.

"Oh, my God. Really Summo, are you that delusional that you think you have a chance?" said Leaf in disbelief.

"Come on guys, you know me. I am a charmer and a good-looking rooster," said Summo, sounding very full of himself.

"Have you thought about what you are saying in front Ahren, who happens to be Selina's mentor, associate, and otherwise somewhat of a father figure to her?" chimed in Spence.

"Oh," said Summo, who had just realised what had come out of his mouth. He slowly raised he his head to look at the hulking man straight in his eyes, and much to his surprise, Ahren had a big toothy grin on his face, as he tried not to laugh again.

Summo could see that he had a silver tooth smack bang right at the front on his bottom tooth line. "I take it you smiling is a good thing?" asked Summo very shy.

"First thing, I find it very amusing, Mr. Summers, that you think you have a chance with my young protégé, and second, she has taken a vow of celibacy."

"Celibacy," repeated Summo very slowly.

"You understand the meaning of celibacy, don't you Mr. Summers?" asked Ahren.

Summo was just standing still with an expressionless look on his face. Spence, meanwhile, was laughing loudly at his mate. He found the whole situation quite amusing.

Leaf, on the other hand, was already over what was going on, and instead eager to know why Ahren had revealed himself to them.

"I take it you being here, Ahren, means that we need to head back to the hotel?" asked Leaf.

"Yes Mr. Brodie, Miss Delacruise wishes to discuss the situation regarding your parents," answered Ahren. The way Ahren spoke was so formal, it was completely different to what the three mates had been used to hearing only moments before.

EIGHTEEN

"Well, what are we waiting for?" said Spence. "We need to get back to the room pronto."

"It was nice to meet you, Ahren," said Leaf.

"It's my pleasure to make the acquaintance of you three young gentleman. Especially you Mr. Brodie, I feel that you have a long-winded journey ahead of you. And remember gentleman, I will be watching when no one else is," said Ahren.

"Thank you, Ahren," said Leaf. "I feel better knowing we have you watching our backs." The other two nodded in agreement with Leaf's words.

The three mates had gotten about ten meters away from Ahren, when he called out, "Make sure you tell Miss Delacruise to lay off the cigarettes. Leaf threw a thumbs up above his head as they jogged off away from Ahren and the beautiful Mariel Bay.

They retraced their steps back through the streets towards the hotel at a brisker run than they had done earlier. Leaf forged out ahead of his two mates, as he really wanted to hear what Selina had organised regarding his parents' safety.

He opened the hotel room to find Selina sitting in an armchair with a cigarette in her mouth.

"Ahren said you need to lay off those," stated Leaf.

Selina smiled. "He has been telling me that for years. It is starting to sound like a broken record player."

"Well, clearly he has your best interests at heart," followed up Leaf.

"My life, my choice," Selina replied with gusto.

"Either way, I am back because Ahren said that you need to talk to me about my parents," said Leaf.

Before Selina had a chance to respond, Spence and Summo entered the room and Summo blurted out, "Oh my God, he is a massive bugger, isn't he Selina?"

"Yes, he is a massive bugger, as you put it," responded Selina.

"He spoke with so much respect to us," remarked Spence.

"He speaks that way because he was raised in a very strict house in Germany, but don't let the way he talks fool you, he is literally a living, breathing, walking weapon," warned Selina.

Leaf was frustrated by the interruption that his mates had caused him, as he was keen to know about his parents' wellbeing.

"Anyway, before we were interrupted," said Leaf, peering at his mates, "we were going to discuss my parents' safety."

Spence and Summo felt quite sheepish under Leaf's gaze; they both knew how anxious he was.

"Sorry mate," said Summo.

"I am sorry too," said Spence and you could hear the empathy in their voices as they spoke.

"Leaf, you need to take some deep breaths and calm down," said Spence.

"Calm down!" yelled Leaf. "You want me to calm down when I have put my parents at risk of being harmed. Do you understand that?"

"I am an orphan, remember Leaf, so no, I don't know what that means. And think about Summo, he only has his dad left," said Selina sternly.

Leaf suddenly felt awful. He had gotten so wrapped up thinking about himself and his parents, that he didn't think about any of the others' circumstances.

"I am really sorry guys, I didn't mean to be so insensitive and self-centred," said Leaf.

"It's all right," said Summo with a polite smile.

"Getting back to the original matter at hand," said Selina. "First thing is, you need to give me another twenty thousand dollars."

"Why?" questioned Leaf suspiciously.

"Two people means twice as much money. Plus, your dad works on the road as a truck driver, so it would be impracticable for just one person," justified Selina.

"Well, that makes logical sense to me," agreed Spence, as Leaf whipped out his phone and transferred the money across to Selina's account. "All yours," he announced, and Selina responded with a nod and a smile.

"Can you please tell me now, who you have entrusted with my parents' lives?" asked Leaf.

"Yes, I can," said Selina. "The first person, the one who will watch over your mother, is Elena Torli, a Swiss national who is proficient with the Swiss traditional weapon the baselard," explained Selina.

"Baselard? What in blue blazes is a baselard?" questioned Summo.

"Another name for it is a Swiss degan," answered Selina.

"Degan," repeated Summo.

"It's a dagger," said Selina, dumbing down the explanation for Summo.

"Okay, that sounds reassuring to me," said Leaf.

"What about my old man?"

"Well, my first choice for your dad was unfortunately unavailable due to being on another job, however the good news is that I have someone else that I really trust and I know will keep him safe: Mikhail Balashov, who is from Russia," said Selina.

"How will someone with a Russian accent fit into a small Aussie country town?" questioned Spence.

"Mikhail is extremely well versed in mimicking different accents, so there will be no problem for him to blend in," answered Selina.

"Does he have a weapon of choice like Elena's baselard," said Summo sarcastically.

"Mikhail is quite partial to the AK-47," answered Selina, ignoring Summo's sarcasm.

"Really, an AK-47?" said Summo in surprise.

"Yes," said Selina, "an AK-47."

Leaf had a concerned look on his face.

"Is it a good thing that he has an AK-47?" question Spence.

"It all depends what the situation calls for," said Selina jovially, trying to lighten the mood for Leaf.

Summo walked over and put his hand on Leaf's shoulder. "This is all good news mate," he said with a comforting smile.

Leaf felt a lot better knowing that his parents would have someone watching them and keeping them safe. He gave a half-hearted smile back to Summo, still feeling a little uneasy.

Spence could sense that Leaf was still feeling quite uneasy. "Have a look at Selina over here, she clearly is exceptional at her job and takes it seriously. Do you think she would put her reputation at risk by recommending two people that didn't meet her high standards?"

Spence's words made Leaf feel a little bit better knowing how logically Spence's brain was wired.

NINETEEN

"Now that we have your parents' safety well and truly under control, we need to move on to our own state of affairs," said Selina.

"Our state of affairs is that we need to get to that Café and ask questions about the belt buckle," said Summo in a condescending voice.

Selina looked back at him with daggers in her eyes. She was not impressed with his words one little bit. She took a deep long breath before she spoke. "Seeing as you are trying to be the brains of the operation, that doesn't seem like a very detailed plan at all. How do we get their safely? Do we all go or only a couple of us? Can we trust the people that work there? And that's not to mention what will happen if our friend Tamina manages to find us. Hmm."

"Ah... um," was the only response that came out of Summo's mouth. He clearly had not put one ounce of thought into any of those details.

Selina had properly put Summo back in his place and stopped him from speaking that way towards her again.

"You're the expert at this Selina. I am sure you have already thought of a plan," said Spence.

"You know I really do like how your head works most of the time, Spence," said Selina.

"Was that a backhanded comment?" he asked.

"No, it isn't. Truth is, no one can think the same as someone else, or even perfectly for that matter," explained Selina.

"I would take that as a compliment mate," said Leaf with a wry grin.

"The first thing we have to do is check out and go to an Airbnb," said Selina.

"Why do we need to do that?" asked Spence.

"If you haven't noticed, I am a female, and sharing a room with you three guys isn't the most comfortable thing for me. Plus, it's not the norm around here," explained Selina.

You could see the three of them drop an "oh" sound simultaneously.

"Get yourselves sorted. We are out of here in ten at the most," commanded Selina, as they all scrambled around and threw everything they had out into their backpacks, ready to leave.

"Where is the Airbnb?" asked Summo.

"Not far," answered Selina. "Just a short walk away. Maybe ten minutes at the most."

They started their trek towards the Airbnb, and it was still a lovely day to be out and about. After about ten minutes, they arrived at their destination: a two-storey building that was a light pale blue colour.

"Here we are," announced Selina. "Make yourselves at home for the next couple of days."

"A couple of days?" repeated Spence.

"Yes, a couple of days," replied Selina.

"Why?" followed up Spence, but before Selina answered Spence, she suddenly said to Summo, "What are you doing?"

Summo was waving his head this way and that, looking at the tops of buildings.

"Ahh, nothing," he replied sheepishly.

Selina just shook her head. "You know you will never see him," she said.

"Are you serious, Summo?" said Leaf in disbelief. "Ahren is trained to be like a ghost."

"Let's get inside. I need to have a shower and clean myself up after my run this morning," exclaimed Selina.

It was a nice spacious open living area that greeted the four of them, and Selina made her way straight upstairs, where they presumed the bedrooms and the bathroom would be located. The three lads flopped themselves down on a couch and armchairs, respectively.

"What now?" asked Summo.

"From the sounds of it, we need to make ourselves at home for the next couple of days," said Spence.

"What do you think about all this, Leaf?" asked Summo.

"Selina clearly has a plan and we just need to trust her," answered Leaf casually.

"Do you think we can trust her, even after she didn't tell us about Tamina?" questioned Summo.

"One thing I know she cares about more than money is her reputation, and I don't think she would let anything damage that," answered Leaf. "Either way, I am going to pick a bedroom and chill out for a bit. I feel like some alone time."

"Hey Summo, you want to check the rest of this place out?" asked Spence.

"You know I do," said Summo with a wink and a smile.

Leaf made his way down the hallway of the two-storey house to a bedroom, and just as he was about to go inside, he saw Selina exiting hers with a change of clothes on, rubbing her hair dry with a towel.

"Feel a bit more normal now?" asked Leaf.

"Yes, thank you. There is nothing like a hot shower to refresh you and warm your body up," answered Selina.

"I know you have a plan, and I just wanted to let you know that I trust you," said Leaf.

Selina was a bit taken aback by his comment; she clearly wasn't expecting to hear it from him.

"I am glad you trust me, but it really doesn't matter if you do or don't. I am here to keep you alive, and that's what really matters," explained Selina.

Leaf smiled. "I know. I understand that now, but I still have one more question about your plan."

Selina twitched her mouth as she thought about what to say. Eventually, she huffed and said, "What is your question?"

"I want to know how we are getting back to Havana," said Leaf. "I get the feeling that we are not going back via car."

Selina smirked. "You would be correct about that. We will go back via the sea on a boat," she explained.

Leaf's sudden big smile filled up most of his face, as he began to look like the cat that ate the canary.

"What is so entertaining about going via boat?" inquired Selina.

"Oh, I have to be there when you tell the other two," said Leaf excitedly.

"Okay, I will bite. Why?" said Selina.

The smile obviously wasn't leaving Leaf anytime soon. "They both get sea sick," he clarified.

Selina grinned back. "I think I can wait to tell them when you are there," she said rather eagerly.

"Excellent," said Leaf. "I am going to spend some alone time and try to relax."

Leaf looked out of the window where he had a beautiful view of the deep blue bay with the sunshine bouncing off the gentle waves. He had to pinch his left arm just to confirm that he wasn't dreaming. If someone had told him about a month ago that he would be looking out over Marial Bay in the picturesque country of Cuba he would have queried their sanity.

He opened the window to feel the cool breeze sweeping off the bay, and he just stood there for a few minutes taking it all in. Then he took a deep breath and lay on the bed, just listening to the breeze gently blowing through the open window, as he slowly drifted off into an afternoon siesta.

TWENTY

Leaf woke up to banging, yelling, and groans coming from downstairs. He quickly jumped to his feet and hustled down the stairs as fast as his legs could carry him. He was hoping they hadn't been somehow discovered by Tamina.

What he found, however, was nothing like what he had expected. Everything in the lounge area had been pushed to one side of the room, leaving a massive open area in the middle, and from what he could make out, his mates were attempting to fight Selina, although they were failing miserably.

"Summo, Spence, what the hell are you two doing!?" yelled Leaf, interrupting the commotion.

"Hey there mate," said Spence calmly, while lying flat on his back on the wooden floor, trying to catch his breath. Selina had her back to Leaf, and when she turned around, she had a massive grin on her face.

"Anyone going to answer my question?" asked Leaf again, still very confused by the situation.

"I had an idea, Leaf," said Summo. "If the worst case scenario should come about, we need to be able to protect ourselves."

"Selina kindly volunteered to teach us some basic Aikido techniques," added Spence.

"I bet she did volunteer quite quickly," said Leaf. "And by the look of the smile on her face she is having a lot of fun kicking both your backsides."

"Ah, that is where you are wrong, Leaf. Remember what I told you about Aikido? There is no kicking involved," corrected Selina.

Leaf nodded his head. "I remember. But more importantly, have you been able to teach them anything?" he enquired.

"I can definitely tell you one thing: they know how to land on their backs extremely well," said Selina with a jovial laugh.

"In our defence," explained Spence, "we haven't been training for that long."

"Training," repeated Leaf with a laugh. "If you call making best friends with the floor 'training,' you must be delirious."

"Well, how about you step up to the plate?" enticed Summo, whose pride seemed to have taken a dent.

"Hmm, how about I observe for a bit before I fall on my backside multiple times?" commented Leaf.

Spence picked himself up off the floor and stood back next to Summo ready to have another tussle with Selina.

Selina stood in the middle of the room and got into position ready for them to approach her. She put out her flat palm facing upwards, and then curled her fingers back towards her palm, basically motioning for them to bring it on.

Summo advanced at Selina and she grabbed his arm and spun her body, using his momentum until he was flat on his back and she was holding his arm and twisting it.

Summo let out a little "yelp" in pain from the way his arm was rotated.

"Do you yield?" asks Selina.

"Yes, yes… I give up!" answered Summo in pain. Selina released his arm and he got up and moved it around, trying to get rid of some of the soreness and tension.

Leaf found it quite amusing seeing Summo being swung around like a rag doll.

Next, Selina looked at Spence. "Are you ready to go again?" she asked.

Spence had been observing what happened with Summo, as well as everything that had gone on in their previous attacks. This time, he moved cautiously towards Selina, not wanting to give her any momentum that she could use against him.

They just circled around each other a few times, like wild animals would circle a wounded prey. Then Leaf yelled out "boring" like a school kid, mocking them to do something for his enjoyment. Selina turned and looked at him, and in the same moment, Spence made his move on her. However, quick as a wink, the same thing happened to Spence as it did Summo, and he found himself flat on his back with his arm being yanked.

Selina helped Spence up off the ground. "You had the right idea, you know?" said Selina, complementing him on his efforts.

"I just can't get over how quickly you move your body, especially the way your hips snaps like that," said Spence.

"Do you care to try, Leaf?" asked Selina, enticing him from the sidelines.

"Um, no. I don't have the urge to feel like a rug getting dusted on the floor, I must admit," he responded.

"Then how do you propose we learn some of Selina's Skills?" asked Summo.

"Easy," said Leaf. "How about we watch Selina's movements and we can copy her? That way we get fewer bruises."

"I like that idea a lot," announced Summo excitedly.

"That sounds like a great idea mate," agreed Spence, rubbing his arm.

"How does that sound to you, Selina?" asked Leaf.

"I can try to make it work, I guess. Although none of this is in my job description," she responded cheekily.

The three lads craned their heads at Selina; they knew it would be hard for them, but they were athletes to some degree. Then, much to their surprise, Selina burst out laughing at them. "You should all see the looks on your faces!" she said, trying hard to stop laughing at them.

It wasn't long before Leaf could see the funny side of Selina's comment and found it nice that she was showing more of who she is a person to them.

"All right, if I am going to show you some basic techniques, you will listen and do precisely as I say," commanded Selina in a very dominant manner. "I am looking at you Dean. No smart-arsed comments," she added, staring him down.

It was clear she meant business because she called Summo by his real name. Summo stood there like a statue and swallowed hard to stop himself from spitting out a wise crack, while Spence almost started laughing at his mate's reactions. If it wasn't for Selina eyeing him down, Spence would have burst out laughing.

"Everyone line up horizontally so you all have a clear view of me and can shadow my movements," ordered Selina, and the three lads hurried into line, as she slowly showed them the way they should move their bodies to use their opponent's momentum against them.

They practiced this for about an hour, with Selina explaining how important repetition is when learning the techniques properly. After that, she showed them the right way to put their hands on their opponent's arms to transition in with a body movement they had just learnt. They were trying to mimic her every movement to their best of their abilities, and they weren't doing too badly at all.

TWENTY-ONE

"I am quite surprised at how quickly the three of you are picking up these techniques," exclaimed Selina, causing the three mates to smile broadly at the compliment.

"When can we throw each other around then?" asked Summo enthusiastically, looking at Spence.

"None of you are close to being able to use these techniques properly against anyone yet," explained Selina sternly.

"Why not?" whined Summo, who was very keen to put someone else on their back after having it happen to him so many times already.

"Because I said so. I am training you, and I am telling you that in no way, shape, or form are you ready yet," commented Selina.

Summo was about to reply but Selina got in first. "End of Story," she said firmly, and Summo decided to keep his mouth shut as it was obvious that he would not be able to change Selina's mind.

"Anyway, I am going to get any early night," stated Selina. "I would advise you all to do likewise. Training starts at seven sharp."

"Seven sharp!" moaned Summo, who wasn't a morning person at the best of time.

"It's up to you, but if you want to actually be able to use these techniques, you must practice them until they become second nature," explained Selina.

Summo took a deep breath and replied in a grumpy voice, "I will be up."

Spence whispered to Leaf, "He must really want to put one of us on our arses to get up that early in the morning."

Leaf smiled back, finding the banter quite amusing, but it was good to see Summo taking it seriously.

"I am going to take Selina's advice and get an early night," claimed Spence.

"I am definitely ready to go to bed as well," stated Summo.

"Yeah, you need your beauty sleep," teased Spence.

"Hey, do you know how hard it is to keep looking this good all the time?" said Summo with a wink.

"Clearly you must have hit your head on the floor when I put you on your back," chimed in Selina.

"Hey, what's that supposed to mean?" asked Summo.

"What that clearly means is that she doesn't think you are as hot as you think you are," teased Spence.

"Ah, so she thinks I am hotter than I really am," said Summo, and the other three almost fell over laughing at what came out of his mouth.

"He must have a concussion. That is the only explanation there can be for that level of delusion," claimed Leaf.

Not long after and Leaf was in his bedroom, looking out of the window at the bay view, with the full moon magically lighting up the night sky. A knock came at the door and Summo let himself in.

"Hey mate, I can't sleep," he said. "What are you doing?"

"Taking in the beautiful view," replied Leaf.

"There's an amazing moon tonight," commented Summo.

"Yeah, there bloody is," agreed Leaf.

"The first moon I saw after my mum passed, my old man told me it was Mum shining down brightly on us from heaven to check in on us," said Summo.

Leaf gave his mate a smile. "If she is checking in on us, I am glad it's her beautiful soul," he said kindly.

"Thanks mate," said Summo. "I think I will try to get to sleep again seeing as we must be up at seven."

Leaf lay in bed trying to get comfortable, but he was finding it hard to fall asleep. Between the recent time zone changes and the siesta he had earlier, his body wasn't ready to rest for the night.

He decided to get up, put some clothes on, and go for a stroll in the clear moonlight of Cuba. It was a brisk night on the streets, and he felt as if the moon's rays were leading him somewhere, as he headed down towards the bay. When he arrived, he could see the moonlight shimmering on the water.

"The bay looks amazing at night in the moonlight, doesn't it?" said a loud voice in the darkness.

It was Ahren. He had followed Leaf since he left the Airbnb.

"I thought you would have followed me down here," said Leaf.

"Wouldn't be doing my job if I didn't," replied Ahren.

"Plus, I would have missed out on this amazing sight and I thank you for that, Mr. Brodie."

"Ahren, how did you end up with a job like this?" asked Leaf. "The way you talk doesn't fit with it somehow."

"Never take someone at face value," scolded Ahren. "And if you must know, Mr. Brodie, I grew up in a strict military family. I followed in my father's footsteps and ended up in the KSK. Then, once I got out of there, I fell into this line of work and have been protecting clients ever since," he went on.

"What is the KSK? I have never heard of it before," asked Leaf.

"KSK stands for Kommando Spezialkrafte, which is the name for the German special forces," explained Ahren.

"Oh, okay. So it's basically for only the best soldiers then," said Leaf.

"That is correct, Mr. Brodie."

"Then how does Selina fit in with this, and with you?" questioned Leaf.

"Ah, Miss Delacruise. She is an interesting person, with an even more interesting background," explained Ahren.

"Interesting how?" asked Leaf.

"Mr. Brodie, Miss Delacruise's story is hers to tell, not mine, and I would be doing her a disservice by not letting her tell it in her own words," explained Ahren.

"I can respect that," said Leaf.

"Thank you, Mr. Brodie. I would recommend that you head back to the house to get some rest now," replied Ahren.

When Leaf got back to his room, he was out like a light, and he didn't wake up until the morning when he heard Spence's voice saying, "Leaf, come on mate. It's time to get up. You don't want to be late."

Leaf slowly dragged himself out of bed and down the stairs, where the other three were already waiting for him.

Selina looked peeved. "Can't you tell the time? Don't answer that," she snapped. "Just get in line with the others."

Leaf quickly made his way over to his mates.

"Now that everyone is finally here," said Selina looking straight at Leaf, "we need to keep practising what we learnt in yesterday's training."

The three mates practiced the same body movements and grabs with each other for hours, while Selina stood there watching them very closely and monitoring how their techniques were improving.

A few hours passed and they were working up a good sweat with their practice. "Okay, you take a break boys," instructed Selina. "I think you have earned maybe ten minutes."

The three of them all grabbed some water and gulped it down in a hurry.

"Do you think we are improving?" asked Spence.

"Yes, all three of you are making slow progress, which is very pleasing," answered Selina.

"Slow," spluttered out Summo.

"Yes, you heard me, unless you have suddenly developed a hearing impairment," replied Selina, and Summo screwed up his face like a spoiled little child.

TWENTY-TWO

Selina wasn't happy with the sour puss look Summo gave her. "Are you ready to step up to the plate again?" she coaxed, "or are you going to make another stupid decision like Leaf did last night?"

"What does she mean mate?" asked Spence.

"Yeah," continued Selina, "explain your actions."

Leaf was left feeling speechless after Selina called him out in front of everyone.

"Seeing how a cat has your tongue, how about I explain it to the rest of your buddies?" said Selina. "Last night Leaf went for a nighttime walk, meaning that Ahren had to follow him, so no one was watching us while we slept."

Summo and Spence looked at Leaf with disappointment on each of their faces. Leaf hadn't thought about what his actions could have meant for the others.

"I am sorry guys, I wasn't thinking. I just couldn't sleep," explained Leaf.

"That's the problem," said Selina, raising her voice. "You didn't think, and from now on you need to think about your actions and how they affect everyone else."

"Look, I'm really sorry," repeated Leaf.

"Sorry doesn't cut it," replied Selina. "Sorry wouldn't help if you came back and we were all dead because of your selfish behaviour. I don't even want to look at you at the moment," she scolded. "I thought you were smarter than that and understood the dangers involved in this."

"I do," said Leaf in a soft tone.

"I am out for a bit before I punch you in your stupid face. Ahren can babysit you for a while!" yelled Selina, walking out of the door.

There was nothing but dead air in the room for a few minutes, as the three mates just stood still, not knowing what to do or say.

Then the front door opened and Ahren came ambling in, shaking his head at them.

"Back in line now, gentleman," commanded Ahren in a loud voice. "Now, show me what Miss Delacruise has been teaching you," he followed up.

None of them argued with Ahren as they started practicing their techniques, while he walked around them, eyeballing every movement they made without saying a single word. The three of them felt nervous in the presence of this hulking German who was being so silent.

Leaf looked at Ahren and their eyes briefly locked together. He could see an intensity that he had not seen before, and it told him that the man meant business. Leaf was going to say something, but after seeing Ahren's eyes, he refocused on what he was doing.

Summo was the first one to decide to say something. "Ahren, how much longer do we have to keep doing this for?" he questioned.

When Ahren didn't respond, Summo looked at him and he could see the same intense gaze Leaf had seen a few minutes ago. Summo wisely took a long deep breath and just kept going with the training.

After about another hour, Ahren finally spoke. "That's enough for today gentleman, get yourselves some water and clean up."

"Damn, this is harder than I thought it would be," Summo complained to Leaf and Spence. Unfortunately, he spoke too loud and Ahren overheard him.

"Back in line now, gentleman," demanded Ahren, and the three mates gave a big collective groan.

Ahren stood in front of them looking down at them with his hulking arms crossed. "Gentleman, I take training very seriously. You may need to use what we are teaching you to save your lives one day, so I would think about that for a minute. If we train you incorrectly, you could end up no longer breathing," he explained sternly. "This is how I was taught, this is how Selina was taught, and this is how you will be taught too," he continued. "Dismissed gentleman," was his final command to the three tired mates.

The lads slowly trudged up the stairs, their bodies suffering, and their minds feeling worn down. Summo and Spence went off to each of their rooms, and Leaf heard them flop loudly onto their beds.

He made his way to the bathroom, where he had a nice hot shower to relax his tired body. He stood under the warmth of the shower and let his mind clear itself so he could properly unwind. A little while later, his shower was interrupted by someone banging loudly on the bathroom door.

"Yeah!?" he yelled out.

"You have been in there long enough!" came the loud, annoyed voice of Selina.

"Give me a minute," Leaf called back, as he dried himself off and wrapped the towel around his waist, before opening the door. Selina was standing there waiting for her turn in the shower. She looked a lot calmer now than when she had stormed out of the house.

Leaf was about to say something but Selina spoke first. "I know what you're going to say and sorry doesn't help. Like I told you earlier, just learn from your mistakes."

Leaf was again about to say something when Selina cut him off once again. "Look, I am not in the mood to argue. I want a shower, and if you don't move, I'll whip the towel off your waist and embarrass you," she said gruffly.

With that, Leaf hightailed it out of her way and off to the security of his bedroom, closing the door, pressing his back flat against it, and letting out a sigh of relief.

After a few seconds, much to his surprise, he noticed that Ahren was sitting on an old wooden chair in the middle of his room.

"I have been waiting for you, Mr. Brodie," said Ahren. "Clearly, you like long showers."

"Um, yeah, I do. My body needed the warmth after all that training you put us through," responded a surprised Leaf. "Anyway, why are you in my room?"

"Miss Delacruise is going to be harder on you than your friends, you must realise," stated Ahren.

"But why?" questioned Leaf, who still had the towel wrapped around his waist and was feeling uncomfortable and unsure of what to do.

"Mr. Brodie, you decided to take this burden on your shoulders when you could have walked away," explained Ahren. "At the end of the day, your friends Mr. Summers and Mr. Blake can walk away if they feel like it, but you can't. You have started something that you have to finish."

"They have been my friends since kindergarten and I know they will stay by my side for as long as it takes," fired back Leaf, standing up for his mates.

TWENTY-THREE

Ahren stood up to leave the room, but before he did, he turned and looked at Leaf. "I will leave you with these words young Mr. Brodie. Everyone has a burden, what counts is how you carry it."

Leaf was feeling cold with just a towel on, and the cool breeze wasn't helping the course either. Once he'd gotten dressed, he felt a lot warmer as his mind contemplated what Ahren had said to him. He decided he would talk to Spence and see what his logical mind would make of Ahren's words.

He knocked on Spence's door but there was no response. He must have been napping after the morning's training. He decided to try Summo's door but encountered the same result.

He sighed and made a move downstairs, where he started rummaging through the fridge to see what he could find to eat. He could hear someone's footsteps coming down the creaky stairs, and he poked his head above the fridge door to see who it could be. It was Selina, having already finished up in the bathroom.

Leaf quickly ducked his head back behind the fridge, hoping that she didn't see him, as he was in no mood for another lecture, seeing as he'd already received two from Selina and one from Ahren recently.

Unfortunately, he was too slow, and she saw him and called out, "I can see you Leaf!"

He popped his head back up and smiled at her to pretend that he was not trying to avoid her, but Selina wasn't amused by his boyish behaviour.

"You know you need to grow a thicker skin to deal with what's in store for you."

"Yeah, I know," replied Leaf quickly.

"So, you're not sulking from your tongue lashing earlier?" asked Selina.

Leaf burst out in loud laughter, much to Selina's surprise.

"What's so amusing?" she asked.

Leaf was trying his best to stop laughing so he could answer Selina's question. After a moment, he finally calmed down from his little laughing fit and said, "That's the last thing I would have thought would come out of your mouth."

"What?" said Selina, looking quite confused.

"Tongue lashing," answered Leaf. "That's so Aussie."

Selina just had a look on her face that said "really Leaf?"

"You know I have been around the world more times than you would have cooked meals, and I have picked up a lot of expressions along the way," explained Selina.

"To be honest," said Leaf, "I was contemplating what Ahren said to me in my bedroom."

Selina looked surprised by this news. "What, you mean he came and spoke to you in your room?" Her face was full-on intrigue.

"It's like I just said, he came to my room to have a talk with me," repeated Leaf.

"Are you going to tell me what he said or do I have to guess?" asked Selina sternly.

"He said that you will be harder on me than the others, and that it was my burden to carry, not anyone else's. He also told me how I should carry the burden," explained Leaf.

"Hmm, very interesting," replied Selina.

"What do you think he was trying to tell me?" asked Leaf.

Selina gave him a little smile. "The message was for you Leaf, not me nor anyone else. You have to figure it out."

Leaf's shoulders dropped and he felt a bit annoyed that Selina and Ahren were talking in riddles. Selina noticed the change in his body language and said, "You better get used to this. Your whole journey is going to seem like one big puzzle if you act like that over such a small thing. How are you going to act when something harder comes along? How do you think the other two will react if they pick up on your body language?" said Selina.

"Hmm, maybe that's what Ahren was talking about. How I carry this burden will not only affect me but others around me," said Leaf out loud.

Selina gave a shrug of her shoulders and tilted her head sideways at Leaf's words. *What does her reaction mean?* thought Leaf. *Was that a hint that I am on the right path?*

His train of thought was broken up by Summo walking into the room, loudly yawing and stretching his arms out wide in the air. "What are you two discussing?" he asked.

"Riddles," responded Leaf in a glum voice.

"I am great at riddles," said Summo with a big smile

Selina burst out laughing. "You?" she said. "You are good at riddles!"

Summo was not impressed by Selina's reaction, and he just stood there with his arms folded and a scowl on his face.

TWENTY-FOUR

"What has an eye but cannot see?" asked Summo excitedly. Leaf had heard this before a couple times and decided to keep his mouth shut. Selina took a few paces and mouthed the question to herself, then she looked at Summo with a sly grin and said, "The answer is a needle."

Summo let a loud groan of disappointment because she was correct.

"What is yours but others use it more than you?" was Summo's next riddle.

Spence had just come down the stairs and heard it. "I know the answer!" he blurted out.

"It's not for you!" snapped Summo, who clearly wanted to stump Selina. Leaf was getting annoyed with what was going on, the answer to his question and a serious conversation having been turned into a childish riddle game.

"The answer is your name!" yelled out a pissed off Leaf.

"I know," said Selina.

Leaf was just about to storm out of the room when Selina yelled out, "Boat!" and he stopped in his tracks, took a deep breath, slowly turned around, and said, "Boat, what do you mean boat?"

Summo and Spence both had confused looks on their faces.

"What are you two talking about boat?" enquired Spence.

"You know, a boat. A thing that floats on water that you can travel on," he answered.

"Oh no… heck no, I am not doing no boat," responded Summo, who had lost a bit of colour from his complexion.

"Come on," continued Summo, "you know I get sea sick."

"Yeah, guys, so do I," said Spence, who was also unimpressed with the situation.

"The plan is to leave here via boat and travel back to Havana," said Selina, completely ignoring Spence and Summo's whining.

"Hello, did you hear what we just said?" replied Summo. "We get sea sick." He glared grumpily at Selina.

"They make tablets to help with sea sickness," replied Selina with a dead pan look on her face.

Spence sighed loudly. He knew that arguing would not change anything. "So what's the plan then?" he said.

Summo threw his hands in the air in frustration, seeing Spence give up so easily.

"Summo, we have to trust Selina, and she is right, they do make sea sickness tablets," said Leaf, trying to reason with his frustrated mate.

"Just give him a couple of minutes and he will come around," commented Spence. "Anyway," he continued. "What else are we going to do other than traveling by boat, Selina?"

"We will arrive in Havana and get the lay of the land before we move forward," explained Selina. Summo stood there, arms crossed, sulking over the fact they were going to travel via boat.

"I have cities but no houses, I have mountains but no trees, I have water but no fish… what am I, Summo?" asked Selina, changing the conversation.

Summo didn't respond, he just stood there, arms crossed, still unamused about the whole situation.

Selina winked at the other two. "Got him. He doesn't know," she coaxed.

This drew a response out of Summo, as he dropped his arms and was about to say something, but for once he didn't speak. You could see the gears spinning over inside his head as he tried to figure out Selina's riddle.

"I don't think he knows," teased Spence, but Summo didn't bite at his mate's barb. He started pacing slowly across the room, mouthing out the riddle to himself repeatedly. He was determined to win.

This turn of events had changed Leaf's mood from wanting to storm out, to enjoying himself watching his mate sweat bullets trying to answer the difficult riddle.

"Tick Tock," teased Selina, pointing to her wrist and pretending she had a watch.

"Ahh!" screamed Summo in frustration. He was clearly stumped by Selina's riddle.

"What's the answer?" asked Summo, who was pretty much conceding defeat.

Selina just smiled back, gloating in her victory.

"Anyone else have the answer?" she asked, looking over at the other two.

Leaf hadn't been thinking about it; he was just enjoying the show. On the other hand, Spence had been trying to figure it out the whole time.

Leaf shrugged his shoulders. "I have nothing."

"I am out as well," announced Spence, shaking his head in defeat.

Selina just gave another big smile and walked away, heading towards the room's exit.

"Oh, come on," moaned Summo, "Don't be that type of person," but Selina just kept walking away, unmoved by Summo's moaning.

Summo was clearly frustrated before, but now it had gotten a whole lot worse.

"Come on, surely between the three of us we can figure out the answer," he stated.

"Mate, I have absolutely no idea," responded Spence.

"Me either," chimed in Leaf.

Summo rubbed his hands over his face, he was utterly bamboozled by the riddle.

"Look on the bright side," said Leaf, "at least it has taken your mind off going on a boat."

Summo dropped to his knees. "Really mate. Not only can't I solve this riddle, but now you have reminded me that I have to go out on the bloody ocean and get sea sick," whaled Summo.

Leaf just smiled and headed off to his room.

Summo looked at Spence and said, "So what do you have to say?"

but Spence also just walked away from his mate. He was just about to go upstairs into his room, when he suddenly yelled out, "Spider!"

Summo just stayed there on his knees in silence, now paralysed with fear too. The others had all just walked away on him, while reminding him of the three things he hated: losing, boats, and bloody spiders.

Just then, Spence gave out a little laugh and yelled, "Joking!" to the fear ridden Summo.

TWENTY-FIVE

The next day, all four were up and about even earlier than usual, getting ready to make their way back to Havana.

Summo was looking like a shade of white that one would normally associate with a ghost.

"You two," said Selina in the direction of Summo and Spence. "Take these tablets." She tossed them a couple of sea sickness tablets, and the two mates looked at each and then swallowed them down whole.

"I really hope these work," said Summo nervously.

"I second that," said Spence, who sounded just as nervous as his mate.

"Come on guys, you will be fine," said Leaf, trying not to laugh at his two mates.

"It's easy for you to say, you're not the one who will be suffering out there on the ocean," complained Summo.

"You guys will be fine," said Selina in a calming voice.

"How can you be so sure?" enquired Spence.

"One, it's my job to keep calm, and two, those tablets are of my own creation," explained Selina.

"Your own creation?" repeated Summo, already beginning to feel sick in his stomach just thinking about the sea.

"Just do me a favour and trust me," said Selina with a smile of reassurance. "Those tablets have never failed."

Some colour started slowly coming back to Summo's face, her words having filled him with a little confidence.

Leaf walked up to Selina and whispered, "Is that true?"

She smiled back at him and replied, "No, but look how much better he seems having heard it. Never underestimate the power our minds have over our bodies."

Leaf just smirked back at her; he had a feeling he was going to enjoy their time on the ocean.

They heard a horn beeping in front of the Airbnb.

"That's our ride to the harbour," announced Selina to the other three, and they all made their way out to where an old banged-up white Ute was waiting.

Spence just stood there smiling at the Ute as the others all jumped in the back. Selina leaned over and whispered to Leaf, "What is going on with Spence?"

Before Leaf could respond, Spence said, "Now, this is more my style. Look at this!"

"Has he bumped his head or something?" asked Selina.

Spence overheard her and said, "Heck, nah. I haven't bumped my head. This here reminds me of being back home on the farm, riding in the back of the Ute."

"Come on farm boy, hop in and let's go for a ride," said Summo, as Spence jumped in the back shouting, "Let's roll!"

They bumped around in the back of the Ute down the dirt roads towards the harbour. When they arrived, it was around 7 a.m. and the water was calm and motionless.

Leaf and Selina got straight out of the Ute, but the other two stayed in the back, both not wanting to go any further for different reasons.

Summo was eyeing the boat nervously and thinking about being on the water, while Spence, for his part, didn't want to leave the Ute behind because it brought back fond memories of home.

Suddenly, Leaf jumped into the back of the Ute and shook Spence out of his trance, looking him in the eye and saying, "It's time to go mate," as he helped him climb down.

"Can you get Summo please Selina?" asked Leaf, and she didn't look happy about it at all.

"Come on, I did say please," said Leaf, trying to convince her.

She just stood there for a moment looking at Summo and shaking her head back at Leaf.

Eventually, she said, "Come on, it's time to go," but Summo remained unmoving. Selina then climbed in next to him and leaned over to whisper into his ear. "You either climb out yourself or I'll throw you out. The decision is yours," she said.

"Hey guys, Selina says she wants to put her hands on me," said Summo happily, as Selina's eyes widened in disbelief.

She was clearly pissed at having been played like that, so she grabbed him by the back of the shirt and tossed him out of the truck.

Summo hit the ground hard, face first, with a thud that winded him for a few seconds, and he coughed and spluttered, trying to regain his breath.

Finally, he said, "Did you two see that?"

"See what?" asked Spence.

"I saw you getting thrown out of the Ute for acting like an idiot," replied Leaf.

"I told you she wanted to put her hands on me," said Summo with a sort of laugh, but his two mates were completely shocked at what had just come out of his mouth.

Selina slung Summo's bag out of the Ute, and it landed fair and square right on his back, causing him to let out a whimper of pain.

"You know your behaviour is way out of line and disrespectful!" scolded Leaf, as the two mates helped him up off the ground.

Selina was still angry with the stunt that Summo had just pulled. "If you ever do something like that again, or imply that I want to touch you in any way, no one will be able to identify the remains of your body," said Selina in a threating voice.

Summo didn't reply, instead just standing there like a statute. Selina then peered over at the other two. "The same goes for both of you as well," she said, and Leaf and Spence nodded back to her with a glimmer of fear in their eyes at this side of her they hadn't come across yet.

"Now, we'd better hurry and catch our boat before it departs without us," said Selina, rushing off ahead of them.

"Why can't you act normal sometimes?" said Spence to Summo once she was out of earshot.

Summo gave him a wry smile back. "You know what, I still get the feeling that she likes me."

Leaf and Spence both gave him a whack in the back of the head simultaneously. "Do you really want to die by keeping our protection furious at us all the time?" asked Leaf.

He took Summo's lack of response as a sign that he understood what he'd said.

"Come on guys, we need to catch up to Selina, so we don't get left behind," reminded Spence, as they walked along the harbour past many different types of boats, including yachts, tug boats, speed boats, and a massive cruise ship. There were even heaps of other boats that the three mates didn't even recognise.

"I hope we get to go on an elegant yacht or a classy speed boat," said Summo.

"Don't get your hopes up," replied Leaf, as they arrived at the industrial part of the harbour, where there were massive stacks of shipping containers everywhere.

Summo let out a sigh of disappointment, as they rounded a massive pile of shipping containers to find Selina talking to a man in front of a huge ship that had been hidden from view.

None of the lads had ever seen a ship of that size and they were literally in awe of it.

Selina came over to them and announced, "This is our ride."

"This is a ship, not a boat," said Spence, pointing out the bleeding obvious.

"Ship, boat, dingy, it doesn't really matter as long as it floats and gets us to our destination," answered Selina.

"Um, Selina, what type of boat is it?" asked Leaf.

"It's an oil tanker," responded Selina. "Is that a problem?"

"No, no not at all. It's more out of curiosity than anything else," answered Leaf.

"How did you organise this?" enquired Spence.

Selina took a deep breath. "You don't think I know a variety of people from around the world in this line if work? Now, enough of the twenty questions, it's time to board."

Summo stood there for a few extra seconds, just looking at the tanker while trying not to think of the waves crashing against it. Then the four of them made their way up a long flight of rusty metal steps, with Spence inspecting the tanker intensely as he walked.

When Selina turned around to check on them, she could see the intense look on Spence's face. "What's wrong?" she asked.

"Just taking everything in," he replied nonchalantly.

They reached the top of the stairs and stepped aboard the tanker, where Selina again asked Spence, "What is going on with you?" She clearly wasn't buying his previous answer.

Her questioning made Spence feel rather nervous. "The tanker does look a little old, and I was trying to make out the name of it."

"Imagine how rough the oceans get and the beating this ship would take from the waves crashing on to it. You would look this old as well," replied Selina. "This tanker is in excellent working condition, and her name is *Maja Linnea*," she continued.

"That's an odd name," chimed in Summo.

"You only think it's odd because it's outside of what you would classify as your normal comfort zone," said Selina.

Summo was about to reply when Selina said she didn't want to hear it.

"What does the name mean?" asked Leaf.

"It's a Swedish-owned ship, so it has a Swedish name. Ships are traditionally given female names too," explained Selina.

TWENTY-SIX

Since boarding the tanker, and while these discussions had been taking place, Summo had just stood there rigidly, holding tightly on to the metal railing with both hands.

The three others suddenly realised this, and they all turned to look at him.

"You okay there, mate?" asked leaf.

"Um, yeah mate, of course," replied Summo, his voice very shaky.

Selina gave a shake of her head at his response.

"Let's go find our quarters," she said, and they all followed her, with Summo at the rear, moving very slowly while keeping hold of the rail the whole time.

"You know we haven't even left the dock yet," teased Spence.

"Let him be," said leaf.

"I don't really want to deal with him being sick the whole the trip," replied Spence.

"He won't be sick. Remember he has taken sea sickness tablets," Selina reminded him.

They moved to the inside of the ship, where everything just felt like a giant metal maze. Going through several doors, up some stairs, down some stairs, they finally got to their quarters, which weren't much more than a small square box with a couple of metal bunk beds that didn't look particularly inviting.

"How long will this trip take?" enquired Spence.

"It all depends what the conditions will be like on the water," answered Selina. "It could take as little as three hours or up to seven."

"It would be fantastic if it were seven," said Spence in a sarcastic tone, just as all four of them lurched backwards with the ships departure.

Summo let out a big worried sigh.

"How about we lie down on our beds for a while?" suggested Spence.

"Yeah, that's a good idea," agreed Summo.

Spence and Summo both lay down on their beds, with Spence on the top bunk and Summo on the bottom.

Leaf was about to leave the small room, when Selina asked, "Where do you think you are going?"

"Um, I was going to have a look around," answered Leaf.

"Oh, I forgot we were here on a holiday. Why don't you go and check out all the sites on the cruise ship?" said Selina in a sarcastic tone.

Summo and Spence just looked at Leaf standing by the door hesitating.

"We stick together, we stay safe. That's the plan. Get your head in the game," said Selina.

"I know we are not on a holiday, but I would like to have a look around. How often in life do you get to travel on an oil tanker?" replied Leaf. "Plus, Ahren is onboard I presume, so we will have eyes on us."

"You are young and eager for new experiences, I get that Leaf," explained Selina. "However, this is not the time nor the place to go exploring."

Leaf was disappointed by Selina's words. "See it from my point of view Leaf, there are too many variables. The ship is a giant maze; a metal box with limited to no phone coverage," she said.

Leaf just climbed up into the top bunk bed without saying a word, and Selina took his silence as an acknowledgement of her point of view.

After a few minutes of silence, it was Summo who spoke up. "What do we do now?" he said.

"What do you think we are supposed to do mate?" answered Leaf, but before Summo could answer, Spence jumped in. "Don't answer that."

"Why not?" questioned Summo.

"Think about what Selina just said to Leaf before," responded Spence.

Summo let out a sigh like a little kid. "What are we going to do until we get back to Havana?" whined Summo, clearly deciding to ignore his mate's advice.

"What would you normally do in this situation?" enquired Selina.

"That's easy, I would be on this magical thing called a phone. Hang on, I can't do that because I don't have one anymore," he carried on like a pork chop.

Suddenly, something landed on Summo's lap that made him jump, and he looked down to see a white box. It was a deck of cards.

"What have you got there?" asked Leaf.

"A deck of cards mate," answered Summo.

"That should keep you three entertained for a while," quipped Selina.

Summo stared at the cards with a confused look on his face.

"I don't know any card games," he said quietly, almost embarrassed by the fact.

Selina rolled her eyes in frustration, having the feeling that she was a babysitter again. "What about you two?" she asked.

Not a peep came out of Leaf or Spence.

"What is wrong with your generation? You have no idea what else there is around you in this world. All you do is stare at your phones and have absolutely no imagination at all," Selina ranted in frustration.

Summo burst out laughing at the way Selina was carrying on, and his two mates stared at him with stunned looks on their faces.

"Why the heck are you laughing at Selina?" said Leaf in shock.

The look on Selina's face clearly suggested that she was going to cause Summo an extreme amount of pain at any moment, but before she had a chance to get her hands on him, he said, "Your rant reminded me of an old man yelling at a cloud."

Leaf and Spence's jaws almost hit the floor in shock when they heard this, but what surprised them even more was that Selina suddenly burst out laughing.

"See guys, I keep on telling you that I am fu—" began Summo, but before he could finish the sentence, Selina grabbed him and pinned him down on the bed with his arm twisted behind his back. She was really wrenching at his shoulder, and you could tell how much pain he was in by the grimace on his face.

After a few more seconds of pain, Selina finally released him. "That was funny, but if you ever call me old, or even imply it, I will end you," she said in a stern voice.

"Come on," said Summo, "you did laugh, you can't deny it."

"If I didn't laugh, I think your arm would be broken right now," responded Selina with a sly smile.

Just then, Leaf stepped in to defuse the situation. "Seeing as us three don't know any card games, I am sure you must have a few you could teach us," he said.

Selina could see what Leaf was doing; she hadn't come down in the last shower. "I know a lot of different card games, but I am not sure if certain people in this room are smart enough to pick them up," said Selina in a teasing manner.

Leaf's face cringed at her words.

"What are you trying to say about us?" snapped Spence.

"No, no, I am not saying that as a group you might not be able to pick up the games, I am saying there is just one of you," replied Selina with a cheeky wink towards Summo.

This time, Spence stepped in to try to stop the back and forth bickering between Selina and Summo. "I always wanted to learn how to play poker. I am sure you would be able to teach me," said Spence.

Selina decided to change tact on the situation as she felt she had proven her point to Summo.

"I can teach you poker, but which version would you like to learn? Five-card draw or Texas hold'em?" asked Selina.

Spence was about to reply, when Selina held her right hand out towards him like a stop sign, looking at him and waiting for him to respond to her question. You could see his brain going into overdrive, trying to choose, but he was also still laughing on the inside at the way she had just treated his mate.

Before Spence could answer, Leaf said, "Which type of poker do you think would be the easiest to teach us?"

There were a few seconds of silence that felt more like minutes, until Selina responded, "Let's start with five-card draw."

TWENTY-SEVEN

They were sitting on one of the bottom bunk beds in a circle, and Selina delt everyone five cards face done.

"Out of the five cards in front of you, you want to choose what you think are the best cards to keep and throw the other ones out. Now let me tell you the best hands," she continued. "Royal Flush Ace, King, Queen, Jack and ten all the same suite. Next is the straight flush, which is five cards in suite sequence, for example seven, six, five, four, and three in Diamonds. The third best hand is four of a kind, which is self-explanatory." As she spoke, she looked at the three mates to see if they understood, and they responded with three quick nods of their heads.

"Next, is the full house…" Before Selina could finish, Summo interrupted her. "I know what a full house is," he said.

"How do you know that?" questioned Spence.

"I saw it on TV once. It's when you have three cards of the same value, and another two of the same value, like three sevens and two twos," said Summo.

Selina gave a slight nod of approval and it looked like the two had finally stopped their silly bickering.

"The flush is next, with five cards of the same suite, then you have a straight. The last couple are three of kind, two pairs, one pair, and lastly, if no one has anything, the winner will simply be the person with the highest card," finished Selina. "Do we have any questions?" she then asked.

"What are we playing for?" said Leaf, who had been unusually quiet for a while. He had been listening to Selina explaining the game, however he was also thinking about what laid ahead of them when they made it back to Havana.

The two main things he had been churning over in his mind, was the hope that they were going to the right place to find the next key, and even more concerning was if they were going to run into Tamina.

"Why do we have to be playing for something?" asked Selina.

"Can't we play for fun?" Summo made a funny face at Selina, but before she could open her mouth and start the bickering again, Leaf said, "Playing for fun would be nice and relaxing."

The four of them sat there and played multiple hands of poker as the time ticked by. Most of the hands were going in favour of Selina, who clearly had the edge with experience on her side.

There was a lot of laughing going on as well, which was mainly aimed at Summo, who had somehow managed not to win a single hand yet. Leaf, Spence, and Selina were so bemused by this fact, and he himself was getting quite animated. He would throw his hands in the air after every hand and he even started muttering to himself.

"How about a couple more hands and then we can go out for some fresh air?" suggested Selina.

"No, no, no," yelled out Summo. "I have to win one hand at least."

"Going outside for some fresh air and a stretch, sounds great to me," said Spence, elbowing Leaf.

Leaf knew that Spence was winding Summo up, and he was going to join in for a bit of fun.

"How about we just stop now instead of playing any more hands?" suggested Leaf slyly.

Summo looked like he was about to blow his top.

"Come on," said Selina, "I said at the start that the game might be hard for some people to win. Let's give him a chance."

Summo's eyes looked like they were going to pop out of his head, until he saw the cards he had in his hand and a small smile came across his face.

"Oh, maybe he has a good hand," said Spence, teasing Summo.

Summo narrowed his eyes and stared down his mate. "I think this should be our last hand," he announced, and the other three raised their eyebrows at him.

"Well someone is very confident," commented Selina, keeping three cards and throwing away two. Leaf and Spence both kept two cards and discarded three. Then their eyes all wandered over to Summo to see what he would do.

Summo kept all five of the original cards he was dealt and gave them a wink with his right eye. He was looking and feeling rather confident with his cards in his right hand.

"You going to show us what you have?" enquired Spence.

"You guys first," responded Summo confidently, still with a smug smile on his face.

Spence had a pair of fours, and Summo's smile got a little bit bigger. Leaf laid down three Jacks, which is an excellent hand, and the two mates peered at Summo, waiting for him to show them the five cards that had made him so confident.

He very slowly put his cards down, showboating his hand off to everyone. Ten, nine, eight, seven, and finally his last card was a six.

"There it is: a straight. The win goes to me," boasted Summo very loudly, jumping up off the bed.

"Wait with the celebration and show some respect. We haven't yet seen Selina's cards," said Leaf.

Selina sat there stone-faced, giving nothing away about the cards she had in front of her. Then, she copied what Summo had just done, slowly putting them out in front of the others. Seven, eight, nine, and then a ten. She held on to the last card and looked at Summo, who's eyes were bulging out of his head.

"What do you think I have?" teased Selina.

Summo didn't answer, and it was like the air had suddenly been sucked out of the room and no one was breathing. Selina gave a wink with her left eye and surprised everyone by handing the card over to Summo to look at.

Then Summo very slowly brought the card up to his eye level, while Selina got up and went over to the doorway.

Leaf and Spence looked at each other sideways; they had absolutely no idea what was going on.

Suddenly, Summo dropped to his knees and just screamed out, "No, no, no! You have rigged this, haven't you Selina?"

Summo looked so upset that he might completely spit the chewy, as Selina stood by the door, not looking very impressed with his childish behaviour.

"How could this be rigged if Spence shuffled and delt the cards?" replied Selina.

"What's the card?" asked Leaf, who didn't get what was going on with these two.

Summo tossed the card onto the bed in disgust and stomped towards the door like a toddler throwing a tantrum. The card landed face up on the bed; it was a Jack, completing Selina's straight, which was only one card higher than Summo's straight.

The two mates both screamed out, "Ohhhh," in unison as they saw the card. They couldn't believe Selina had a Jack, especially seeing as Leaf had already laid out three of them.

They were about to get stuck into Summo, who had stomped off towards the exit, but when they looked up, Selina was shaking her head at them.

They were puzzled by this, especially after all the back and forth arguing that went on between Selina and Summo.

"It's time we get outside for some fresh air and to give our bodies a good stretch," announced Selina, and the four of them weaved their way through the metal maze towards the exit.

It was very quiet within the group, with no one having said a word since they left their quarters. They finally made their way to the outside of the boat, where they were met with a stiff wind whacking them in their faces.

"Phew, that wind has got some bite to it," exclaimed Leaf.

It felt good to be outside with the wind on their faces, feeling the warmth of the sunshine on their skin. It was still a bit odd for the three mates to be on a massive oil tanker in the middle of the ocean, but at least the waves looked like they were barely touching the ship.

"Are you feeling sea sick?" Spence asked Summo.

"Nah mate, I don't feel sea sick; I feel sick about losing that last hand of poker," replied Summo.

"What about you Spence, how you feeling?" asked Leaf.

"All good here mate, those sea sickness tablets Selina gave us are working a treat," commented Spence.

Leaf felt a lot more comfortable being outside; he had started getting a bit edgy being inside a small space for so long. He had still been thinking a lot about what was going to happen once they got to Havana while they had been playing poker.

Selina came up next to Leaf, almost being able to feel how tense he was. "You need to relax. I am here to protect you," she said.

"How do you know that I haven't been relaxed?" asked Leaf.

"It's my job. It comes with the territory," answered Selina.

"What do you mean?" asked Leaf, clearly not understanding.

"I have been trained to read people, especially their body language. It gives me a fantastic understanding of what is going on with them internally," explained Selina with a slight smile.

"How much longer do you think we will be on the water for?" asked Spence.

"I have no idea," said Selina. "But it's great out here. I can't remember the last time I was out on the open seas." She was showing a more human side of herself for a change.

The three mates stood there for a few moments in a bit of shock seeing her let her guard down in front of them.

Selina could tell they had seen something unusual out of her, and she quickly changed tact.

"How about we go and see the captain and ask him how long it will be before we hit Havana?" she suggested.

TWENTY-EIGHT

They made their way towards the wheelhouse, where the captain would be, and then they began heading up a few flights of metal stairs, listening to the clanging sound they made on each step.

They walked into the wheelhouse and found the captain standing there, looking out of a side window with his back to them. He spun around to see who had walked in, and they could see he was all rugged up in a big puffer jacket, a scarf, a beanie, and gloves.

Selina went over and started speaking to him in a language that wasn't English so the three of them had no idea what they were discussing.

After that, she came over with him and introduced them to "Vicente Alvaro Manuel," who shook each of the mates' hands.

Spence asked the captain if he was cold, and he looked back at Spence with a blank expression. Then Selina spoke to him again in another language and he responded in kind.

In English, Selina said to Spence, "He says he gets really cold when he is out on the water."

"I take it he doesn't speak English with a name like Vicente and the way you two were communicating?" said Leaf.

"I speak very good English," answered Vicente in a thick Spanish accent.

Vicente and Selina started have a good old laugh at the expense of the three mates, who had shocked looks written across their faces.

"What the hell is going on here?" said Summo, who was complexed by the situation.

"We were having a joke at your expense," answered Vicente.

"Oh," said Summo.

"It's a good thing we didn't say anything stupid or offensive then," said Spence with a little nervous laugh of his own.

"How much longer until we dock at Havana?" Leaf asked.

Vicente rolled up one of his sleeves, he looked at his watch, then he walked over to a window and had a good look out with a pair of brown binoculars.

"Hmm," said Vicente, rubbing his two-days' growth of beard. "By my rough calculations, looking at the water and weather, about two hours."

"What? Two more hours, really?" whined Summo.

"Come on mate, two hours isn't that bad. You will be fine," said Spence.

"But it already feels like it has been days on this ship," continued Summo.

"You're just whining because you couldn't win a single hand of poker," quipped Selina.

The look on Summo's face was absolutely priceless; if only one of them could have been quick enough to take a pic of his expression, it would have made a hilarious meme.

"So, the next question is, what do we do for the next couple of hours?" asked the thoughtful Spence.

"The answer is clear, isn't it?" responded Summo of all people. The rest of the group stood there in a bit of a shock for a few split seconds.

"Do you care to share your thoughts with the rest of the group?" asked Leaf.

"Well," said Summo, clearing his throat and preparing to take this big moment for him to shine.

"We will dock back in Havana and we need a plan this time," he explained. "Last time, in all fairness to Selina, who didn't know we were being tracked, I don't think we were fully prepared," finished Summo.

Leaf quickly glanced out the corner of his eye to catch how Selina would react, but her face hadn't flinched much to his surprise, given that Summo had a knack for getting under her skin.

Spence made a slight head nod and peered over at Leaf, who nodded his head back in agreement.

Selina exhaled loudly then spoke. "I really hate to say this, but he is right."

Leaf could hardly believe those words had left Selina's mouth; he would have put money on hell freezing over before she would say such a thing. You could also see that Summo himself was taken aback by it.

"This may sound bloody harsh Selina, but Summo is right: you are the expert, and you need to lift your game," said Leaf in a very demanding and authoritarian voice.

His two mates were taken aback by his change in demeanour and tone of voice. This seemed to flick a switch in Selina's brain. "Everyone back down to our cabin… now," she demanded, and the three mates followed her back towards the cabin while she was on her phone texting someone.

They had only been back in the cabin for a moment, when suddenly, the imposing figure of Ahren was standing in the middle of the room.

The big hulking figure was intimidating at the best of times, but standing in that small area made him look twice as big, and to boot he had short black gloves on his giant hands.

"Ahh, what the heck is going on here?" said Spence, looking confused. What was even weirder than that was that there was a chair in front of Ahren with an electric shaver placed on top of it.

Summo's eyes almost popped out of his head as he yelled out, "No!" and spun around to make a swift escape, but unfortunately Selina was blocking his path.

Leaf was a bit slow on the uptake, until he felt the giant hand of Ahren on his shoulder.

"You need to sit down on the chair, Mr. Brodie," said Ahren.

Leaf took a deep breath as he turned around and slowly sat down in the chair, not wanting to upset the hulking man. He sat there in silent waiting for the sound of the hair trimmer to start, expecting to see his black hair falling to the floor at any moment. Instead, he felt something entirely unexpected. It was slightly cold and it reminded him of shampoo or conditioner.

Soon after, there was a massive uproar of laughter coming from his two mates, who almost had tears running down their cheeks. Leaf felt Ahren's massive hands start to massage his scalp, and he gulped hard, totally in the dark as to what he was up to.

The next thing Leaf heard was the sound of scissors clicking around the top of his head. Then he caught a peculiar sky blue colour out of the corner of his right eye. It was then that it finally dawned on Leaf what had happened: Ahren had died his hair from his natural black to sky blue, and he was now cutting away at it.

He felt like jumping out of the chair, but he remembered that Ahren was in the process of cutting his hair. Almost as a sixth sense, Ahren must have felt what was going through Leaf's mind, and he said in a very calm manner, "Mr. Brodie, take a deep breath. Everything is going to fine. You need to trust me."

Leaf sat there very still and did what Ahren had suggested, taking in a long deep breath to settle his nerves.

After a few more moments and couple more snips of the scissors, Ahren announced, "Mr. Bodie, I am finished," as he handed Leaf a mirror to check out his handywork.

Leaf quickly grabbed the mirror, eager see what had happened to the top of his noggin, feeling quite anxious.

As he glanced in the mirror he saw that his once black hair was now sky blue and cut right down to what Leaf could only describe as a buzz cut.

The cut itself, Leaf didn't mind so much, but he couldn't get his head around the colour. Selina then came right up to his face and said, "You need to keep still," while raising up her hand with a small paintbrush held in her grip.

Leaf's eyes were as wide open as physically possible; this all a little too much for him. He suddenly jumped to his feet, knocking Selina to the ground, and said in a highly agitated manner, "What are you two up to?"

Selina was not impressed that Leaf had managed to push her to the ground and she demanded, "Get your arse back on the chair now!"

"No!" replied a very defiant Leaf. "Not until one of you explains what is going on, and what on earth you are doing to me."

"Mate, you need to chill before you blow a gasket," said an impressively calm Spence.

"It's easy for you to say; your hair doesn't look like the ocean, and Selina was about to start painting my face like I was a child at the fair," snapped back Leaf.

"You need to take your emotions out of the situation and really think about it," replied spence, still in a calm voice.

There were a couple of moments of silence and you could feel that tensions were high in the small room, which seemed to heighten it even more.

Ahren stepped from behind the chair and spoke in a very collective manner to ease the tension. "We need to change all of your appearances so that none of you can be recognised by anyone from Reblick."

Leaf let out an "ahh" sort of sound, and said, "You do realise that if you actually communicate your intentions to us, you wouldn't have to deal with me losing my mind?"

You could tell that Selina was over all the talking, as she was standing there with her arms folded and a sort of scowl across her face.

Ahren again took charge of the situation. "Mr. Brodie, if you would be so kind as to sit back down on the chair, we can finish with your disguise."

"Yes, of course I can do that. It wasn't so hard to talk to me, was it?" replied Leaf. "Just two questions: what is the paintbrush for? And surely those two are going to look more ridiculous than me, right?"

A smile spread across the big German's face. "The paintbrush is to help apply the goatee that Selina is going to give you, and you will have to wait to see what they look like," he said with a wink.

This drew the ire of Summo. "What do you think you will be doing to my beautiful hair?" he snapped. Leaf gave his mate a dirty stare and pointed at his own hair, saying, "Really?"

The around about bickering had finally gotten to Selina's last nerve. "Sit down and do as you are told," she demanded.

"You wanted me to be at the very best of my game, well this is what you get," she continued, sounding very agitated.

TWENTY-NINE

Leaf quietly and rather sheepishly went back over to the chair, trying not to make eye contact with Selina, as he did not want to cause any more trouble.

Selina knelt back down in front of him so they were eye to eye and only a few inches apart, and Leaf could see and feel the intensity coming from her eyes, as if it was going to cut through his body.

Before she started with the goatee, she said, "What I am putting on you is a sort of glue to hold it on, so don't move a muscle."

The bristles of the brush and the glue felt very chilly as Selina carefully placed the glue in the correct position. Then she picked up the fake goatee that was about a little finger width all the way around and like a midnight black in colour. It felt really peculiar on his face as he moved his jaw in a multitude of directions so he could get used to it being there.

"Don't touch it with your hands for the next ten to fifteen minutes, Mr. Brodie," cautioned Ahren, "otherwise you will have undone all of Miss Delacrusie's hard work."

Leaf jumped out of the chair, sort of happy that it was over and done with for now. He was even more happy as he looked at his two mates with a cheeky smile, and said, "Who's next?"

Spence calmy strolled over to the chair, sat down, and said, "Ready."

"Well, that was too easy," quipped Selina, and it was Leaf who let out a laugh this time.

"What is so amusing, Mr. Brodie?" asked Ahren.

There was a massive grin across Leaf's face. "Spence wants to get it over and done with because the quicker he's done, the quicker the fun really starts," he said, pointing his finger at Summo, who was standing there looking very anxious, while stroking his styled blonde hair that he cared for so much.

An even bigger smile spread across Selina's face as she realised this was her chance to get one over on Summo for all their back and forth arguing earlier.

Ahren started snipping away at Spence's hair with the scissors and buzzing with a hair trimmer until Spence had a brand-new slick hair style.

Their mate Spence had never looked so different, and they had to admit that they would not even recognise him let alone Reblick.

Spence had a look in the hand mirror, and even he was taken aback by how good his hair looked, as he let out a little "wow" to himself.

Ahren could sense that Spence was quite taken with his handywork and it put a slight smile on his face. Spence's hair was still its natural brown colour, however it was a lot shorter now, and it was styled with a hard trimmed left to right and a sweeping part. It was worlds away from his usual busy brown curly hair that was always untamed.

"You're up next mate," said Spence, jumping up off the chair with a bit of extra pep in his legs from having his new hair style. All eyes were now focused on the one person in the cabin of the three mates who was yet to have his hair changed at the hands of Ahren. However, before Summo could react, something unexpected happened: Selina sat down in the chair in front of the hulking German.

Ahren had the shaver in his hand already buzzing, taking off what short blonde hair she had left. In a matter of minutes, Selina's hair was gone, and she was now completely bald.

Summo fell to his knees on the cabin floor with a couple of tears slowly rolling off his cheeks at the sight, and Ahren and Selina were stunned at his reaction, almost wondering if it was some sort of distraction to escape losing his valuable hair.

His two mates knew different however; there was only one reason that Summo would show this type of emotion, and that had to do with his mum. His two mates quickly came to his side to help him back to his feet, while he wiped the tears away from his cheeks.

"Mr. Blake, are you okay?" asked Ahren with compassion in his voice. Summo tried to speak; his mouth was moving, but no words came out. He put his head in the air, closed his eyes, took a massive breath to fill his lungs, and then he let all the air back out to gain his composure.

Summo went to speak again, and this time some very muffled words came out, with plenty of emotion in every syllable. "The last woman I saw with a bald head was my beautiful mum when she was going through cancer treatment."

A giant lump formed in the other four people's throats in the room. It was very difficult for them to hear Summo speak this way and see him in that sort of emotional state.

Summo finally made his way very slowly towards Selina in the chair, and he reached out with his right arm to touch her bald head. You could tell Selina was uncomfortable by how wide her eyes where; she looked like she was about to move away from the chair.

There were two hands on her shoulders all of a sudden; they were Ahren's. "Let him be," he whispered to Selina, calming his young protégé.

Summo placed his hands on Selina's bald head, then he stroked the top of the crown very slowly, before just lying on the bed without saying a single word. Leaf had never seen Selina look so out of her comfort zone before.

Ahren whispered to Selina, "That is one of the most noble things I have ever seen you do. I am very proud of you."

This time it was Selina's turn to show some emotion as a tiny trickle came out of her left eye. Ahren was not the sort of person to shower anyone with praise at all, let alone say something like that to Selina.

She had waited to hear those sorts of words coming from Ahren ever since she had met the hulking German. It was hard for her to imagine that, out of everything she had done in her life, sitting in a chair to let another human being touch her head would be the reason.

Selina moved her head quickly away in an attempt to hide her tears from Leaf and Spence. Before anyone could say anything else, Ahren started applying glue to the top of her bald cranium. "You need to sit still Miss Delacruise," he reminded her, as he made the last adjustments with the glue.

"Are you ready for your wig now, Miss Delacruise?" asked Ahren, and Selina gave her mentor a slight nod of the head, before he carefully placed the wig on her head, and then handed her the mirror to see his handywork.

What she could see was a very stylish flame red, with short tight winglets that fell down to her shoulders. It was an amazing transformation.

Next, Ahren walked over to the bed where Summo was lying and said, "Mr. Summers, I hate to disturb you, but it is your turn in the chair."

Summo raised himself from the bed and moved over to the chair without any fuss or crazy antics like everyone would usually expect. "Let's get this over and done with," he announced. There was no snipping of scissors to start with for a change, as Ahren was using a comb to change his hair from being slicked back to having a part down the middle.

Summo hadn't moved a single muscle since sitting down in the chair, much to everyone's surprise, especially after the way he was acting before when he was stroking his hair like it was a precious treasure. Ahren picked up his scissors and started cutting parts of his hair and he still didn't complain at all.

After a little bit of hair cutting, although not nearly as much as everyone expected, Ahren took some blonde hair extensions out of a bag, much to Leaf's disappointment.

"What, you're not going to change his hair colour?" he groaned, but everyone just ignored his outcry, as they were far more intrigued by what Ahren was going to do with all the blonde strands.

Then, Ahren started adding the long strands of blonde extensions to make Summo's hair look much longer than before, and he tied it in a long ponytail that stretched down to the middle of his back.

"What have you done?" asked Leaf, who was still disappointed that Summo's precious hair wasn't at all messed up like his.

"Ahem," said Ahren, clearing his throat. "I have attached multiple blonde hair clip extensions around his head to change his look completely."

"This looks fantastic," piped up Summo excitedly, looking at his hair in the mirror. "This was a great idea," he continued. "I can do so many different styles with this length as well. Thank you so much." He shook Ahren's hand happily.

Leaf just couldn't resist launching into a childish outburst. "Has this been a massive joke to everyone here? Those two get really cool haircuts, and I look like complete moron. How does that add up seeing as I am the one paying for everything?" Leaf was outraged and he got up and stormed out of the room.

The other four just stood there stunned, looking at each other and wondering what the hell had just happened.

"Wow, that was something I have never seen in my entire life," said Spence, at last breaking the silence in the room.

"Miss Delacruise, I think it would be best if you went after Mr. Brodie to talk to him and I will stay behind with Mr. Blake and Mr. Summers," suggested Ahren.

"Is that really a good idea?" asked Spence. "We are his mates and we know him better than Selina."

"Miss Delacruise will be the best person to handle this situation Mr. Blake," answered Ahren with gusto.

THIRTY

Selina made her way swiftly through the massive ship's metal maze to catch up with Leaf so she could explain what had just transpired in the cabin. She reached the outside deck and found him right outside the door, leaning over the edge of the railing.

"Leaf," she said, but before she could continue, he blurted out, "Look at me!" with anger written all over his face. "I look like a complete Idiot. Are you happy with yourself?"

"Yes," replied Selina quite calmly.

"Oh, so you think I look good? That makes two of us," responded Leaf in a sarcastic tone.

Selina stood there unperturbed. She was not going to get pulled into a yelling match and draw attention to themselves.

Finally, she responded in very calm and precise tone. "Remember what Ahren told you, Leaf? That this is your burden to carry. Is this immature behaviour how you choose to carry your burden?"

Leaf rubbed his hands over his eyes and then very animatedly pointed at his short, sky-blue hair with his right index finger.

"Hmm," sighed Selina. "Can you please stop and think while I talk?"

Leaf stood there unimpressed, folded his arms together, and raised his eyebrows.

"This will be far from the worst thing you are going to go through, and you will have to act a heck a lot of better than you just did a few minutes ago. Also, Reblick are after you, remember? You are their target. You are the one with the book and all the information. Do you really think anyone that knows you could pick you out of a line up now?" questioned Selina, giving him some home truths.

Leaf drooped his shoulders and waved his arms around in frustration. He understood very clearly what Selina was saying, but he was still not a happy camper with his new appearance.

"Surely you could have made me look different without sticking out like a blue light bulb?" complained Leaf.

"Sometimes the best way is to hide in plain sight, coming from my vast experience," reassured Selina with a friendly smile.

Leaf looked over the whole situation and he knew that he wasn't going to win this argument because she was right.

"We need to get back inside to the others," insisted Selina. "We still have much to plan once we get back to shore."

Selina walked back inside and Leaf slowly trudged behind her, rubbing the top of his head. His hair had never been that short in his life, and it felt weird on his hand, not to mention the way the cold breeze sent shivers through his exposed head.

"Next time I need a change of disguise, how about you make me look good and the other two look like this?" suggested Leaf.

"How about we focus on the task at hand for starters, and then we can talk about it if there is a next time?" answered Selina swiftly.

Back in the cabin, Ahren was speaking to Leaf's mates. "Now you have had a good laugh at Mr. Brodie's expense, it's time to support him through what lies ahead. He has a lot of pressure on those small shoulders of his."

"Ahren, we are fully aware that there is a lot of pressure on Leaf's shoulders, and there is nothing wrong with a good laugh to release some stress," replied Spence.

"As long it's the right sort of laughter, otherwise you will have the current outcome where Mr. Brodie has a big outburst and causes more stress," commented Ahren.

The two mates listened closely to their hulking German protector and nodded in agreement as he spoke.

"When Mr. Brodie returns, we don't bring up his new hair style," said Ahren in a stern voice so they knew he meant business.

Only a few seconds after Ahren had finished speaking, Selina and Leaf walked back into the room. Ahren, being the senior figure of the group, took control of what was going to happen next, while making sure Leaf's two friends didn't cause any further unwanted distractions.

"Ladies and gentlemen, if you could make your way to each of your beds and take a seat, we will progress with our plan once we dock back at Havana," said Ahren standing in the middle of the small room.

The other four made their way to their respective beds to wait anxiously to hear what Ahren would say next.

"Once we dock back in Havana we will have to separate into two groups. If we are being watched, they won't be expecting that," he explained.

"Group *eins* will consist of Miss Delacruise and Mr. Brodie; you will make your way to Café el Runika to make contact with the Runika family. Group *zwei* will be myself, Mr. Summers, and Mr. Blake, and we will make a move to another safe house on the other side of the city, as another measure to keep our enemies guessing about our whereabouts." Ahren looked around the room at the four of them sitting on their beds. "Does anyone have any questions about the plan I just laid out?" he said.

There was silence in the room for a few moments while Ahren's plan seeped into the rest of the group. It was Summo who spoke first, much to everyone's surprise. "Your plan seems to make sense, except for one thing."

"Mr. Summers, the plan is quite simple to follow and shouldn't cause any confusion," responded Ahren.

Summo looked rather sheepish as the rest of the group were staring at him, waiting to hear why he was confused with Ahren's plan.

"I would like to know what *eins* and *zwei* means?" said Summo.

Leaf and Spence looked at each other and spoke in unison. "That's actually a good question."

Ahren let out an "ahh" noise of some description. "*Eins* is one in German, and *zwei* is two," he explained. "Are there any other questions about the plan gentleman or Miss Delacruise?"

There was a collective shaking of heads from the group sitting in front of the hulking German.

Selina rose from the bottom bunk bed to stand next to her mentor.

"When we dock in the next hour or so things will be different – I will be different. The back chat and the questions will not be tolerated. We are in charge." The tone in her voice and the look in her eyes where nothing they had seen or heard before. She wasn't loud, angry, grumpy, or demanding; she was speaking at a normal level, but it was the tone that made them really take notice. It was absolutely clear that she meant business.

Ahren was standing next to Selina with his massive arms folded across his chest, and it felt like his demeanour and energy had changed as well while Selina had been speaking to them.

Ahren spoke after a few moments, giving Selina's words time to soak in. "When we talk, you do as we say; no exceptions," he said in a demanding voice, backing up his protégé and showing that they were standing united.

Eventually, Leaf spoke up. "In the meantime, what are we supposed to do? I am a bit over cards."

"We don't really care what you do as long as you stay within these four metal walls," snapped back Selina. The massive change in her whole demeanour was still sinking into Spence and Summo, evidenced by the fact that neither of them had asked a question or made a smart-arsed remark.

Ahren walked over to the chair that he did his hairdressing on and dragged it across the metal floor, with the metal chair on the metal floor making a horrible screeching sound that caused the three mates to cringe.

He then sat the chair down next to the only exit in the room and parked himself on it.

Summo leaned over and whispered in Spence's ear, "Are we in prison?"

"Nah mate, that's a bit extreme. It's more like detention at school. You should be used to that seeing as you spent quite a bit of time there," he whispered back with a grin on his face.

Summo managed a little smirk. "Yeah, I guess I spent a bit of time in detention," he said.

"You and school never really meshed at all," replied Spence with a little laugh.

That little laugh Spence let out made the other three in the room spin around and stare at him. All eyes were suddenly focused on Spence, and it made him very uncomfortable.

Leaf could see how it was making his mate feel, and thinking quickly, he said, "You were thinking about Summo not being able to win at poker, right?" letting out a laugh of his own.

Spence laughed in agreement, very grateful for the support. Laughing about Summo's inability to win a game of poker changed the mood in the room, which brought a grim look to Selina's face, a look of disappointment to Summo's, and a glare from Ahren to his young protégé.

Spence picked up on the glare Ahren gave Selina, and he thought he might ask a question, but he held back due to the warning about it earlier. Ahren, being an observant person, noticed that Spence wanted to speak.

"Mr. Blake, it looked like you were going to talk but held yourself back?" he said.

"I was going to ask a question, but then I remembered that Selina said no more question, so I didn't," explained Spence.

"Ask your question, Mr. Blake," replied Ahren, much to Selina's annoyance.

"You glared at Selina when Leaf spoke about the poker game, why was that?" asked Spence, while keeping an eye on Selina.

Ahren stroked his well-groomed goatee a few times before responding. "I glared at Miss Delacruise due to the fact that she is very good at card games; and even more so at sleight of hand."

Summo jumped off the bottom bunk bed, almost knocking his head on the bed above, and yelled, "You were cheating!" while pointing at Selina.

Selina glared at Summo, and it was so intense that it caused him to slink back onto the bed.

"Just because I have sleight of hand skills, doesn't mean I have to use them to beat a no hope card player like yourself," scolded Selina.

THIRTY-ONE

Leaf yawned loudly while stretching his arms high in the air, then climbing up to his top bunk, he remarked, "I am going to get some shut eye before we get back to Havana."

"Mr. Brodie, that is a very logical idea. I suggest you other three would do the same," said Ahren.

The three others didn't take it as a suggestion; they just went and did it as if Ahren was commanding them like robots.

Leaf lay there on the top of his bunk bed, and for the first time, much to his surprise, he felt the slow back and forth of the ship traveling through the waves.

The trip so far had been far smoother than he anticipated, which was fantastic as he really didn't want to have to put up with his mates' whining and being sick. He gave another loud yawn, and what he thought was a little blink turned into sleep.

He only realised he had slept when Selina woke him up by shaking his arm with her hand over his mouth. He was quite startled by what was going on, and it took him a while regain his faculties.

He noticed that Selina had one finger up to her lips, indicating him to be quiet, and then her eyes darted a couple of times to the exit, clearly telling him to walk in that direction.

Leaf carefully and quietly made his way down the bunk bed towards the door, where Ahren was still sitting on the chair awake. Leaf turned around to see both of his mates still asleep on their beds, and he got the feeling that he wouldn't be saying goodbye to them.

He got a tug on his shirt from Selina, urging him to keep moving with her, and Ahren stood up very slowly as they made their way to the exit.

Selina moved past Ahren and their eyes made brief contact, then Ahren turned to Leaf, and held out his big right hand towards him. Leaf looked at his hand for a moment and then extended his one out, as they gave each other a small handshake.

Next, Leaf followed Selina closely, as they moved quickly through the massive ship. It almost felt to Leaf as if Selina had been on this vessel before, as she seemed to start turning corners before they were even close to them.

Leaf felt like yelling out a couple of questions, like have you been on this ship before, and where are we going, but he didn't, as he didn't want to rock the boat after the big speech about doing as you're told and not asking questions.

They eventually came to an exit at the top of the ship, and he felt a cold shiver up his spine, the wind having picked up since they were outside earlier in the day.

He peered around the top of the oil tanker to get his bearings, and he noticed that they were probably only a few minutes away from docking at the harbour in Havana.

He took in the view and inhaled a deep breath of fresh air. As he exhaled, he felt a slight tap on his left shoulder, and he spun around and saw that it was Selina, motioning for him to keep following her with head and eyes movements, just like back in the cabin.

Leaf nodded back to her then followed her across the deck until they came across some wooden rectangle crates. Leaf stood there looking at the three crates in front of him with a rather perplexed expression. He was just about to ask Selina what was going on, when she spoke first.

"I need you to get into that crate," she said, pointing to the middle of them. Leaf looked at her then looked back at the crates; it appeared as if there was just enough room for maybe two people to fit inside them at a squeeze.

He turned back to Selina and shook his head defiantly, indicating that he was not getting into what felt to him like a coffin.

Suddenly, Selina grabbed him and twisted his arm behind his back in what seemed like the blink of an eye. She leaned right up to his ear, and whispered, "You need to hurry up and get into the crate before anyone sees us. I will be right next to you inside there."

Leaf took another deep breath, feeling extremely anxious about the idea, and Selina released his arm and gave him a little nudge forward.

Leaf slowly slid over one of the edges of the crate and carefully laid down inside. Selina then did the same until they were both now lying in the crate, shoulder to shoulder, staring straight up into the afternoon sky.

Leaf was lying there in a state of anxiety, wondering what was going to happen next, when suddenly the lid was being placed on the crate. He instinctively put both his hand up to protect himself, but before he could stop the lid, Selina put her arm across his body.

Then, just as the wooden lid was about to be sealed, the friendly face of Vicente, the ship's captain, appeared, and he said, "You two all good?"

Selina gave him a quick wink back, and he slowly closed the lid, leaving nothing but little rays of sunshine squeezing through the cracks.

There was basically no room to move at all inside the crate, and Leaf couldn't help thinking that this must be what it feels like to be in a coffin. He still did not know what was going on, as Selina had not told him anything thus far.

He decided to squirm around a bit to see how much actual space there was, while eliciting some sort of reaction from Selina, who was squashed in right next to him.

His squirming indeed got the desired reaction, when Selina whispered, "You need to stay still."

Leaf in turn whispered back, "What the heck are we doing inside of this thing?"

Selina let out a huff, obviously not happy with the way Leaf was behaving so far.

Leaf wasn't impressed by Selina not answering his question either, so he moved his right shoulder into her to force a response. "I told you already that we need to be still!" Selina whispered, but this time in a louder voice filled with frustration.

Leaf was about to reply, when there was suddenly a lot of noise happening around the crate, causing him to keep his trap shut for now. He could hear Vicente shouting loudly at someone, but he couldn't make out any words as he was speaking in his native language, Spanish.

After a while, Vicente's voice faded, along with the other noises that had been happening around them, and suddenly they lurched and Leaf experienced a sense of weightlessness that was highly uncomfortable. He grasped at anything he could get his hands on, but the only two options were the floor or Selina's arm.

The feeling of having no control over their movements was gripping Leaf with fear, and Selina could sense this in his hard grasp on her arm.

Much to Leaf's surprise, she put her hand on his leg, tilted her head closer to his ear, and whispered, "Everything is going to be okay."

Leaf took a couple of deep breaths to try to calm his nerves, closed his eyes tight, then sucked in a couple more breaths. "It's going to be okay," repeated Selina, still trying to comfort him.

Leaf responded this time. "Can you please tell me what is going on? It will really help me."

"Just wait a few more moments and then we can talk freely," explained Selina, as they felt the bottom of the crate hit something hard, jolting them and bouncing them off the lid.

Leaf was at the end of his tether by now and was about to lose it and let out a frustrated scream. The only thing that stopped him was the familiar voice of Vicente talking to them in Spanish. Selina responded in Spanish in her normal tone of voice, then she said, "Give it about ten to fifteen minutes and will be out of this box."

"Fifteen minutes!" repeated Leaf. "That gives you enough time to explain this entire situation."

Selina held her breath for a few seconds, gathering her thoughts before she responded. "We are in a wooden crate on the back of a small truck, and Vicente is driving us to a safe place to get out, so we can return to Havana undetected," she said.

Just then, there was an unexpected noise, and Leaf knew it was unexpected by the weird blank look that was written all over Selina's face.

THIRTY-TWO

They both lay there in silence, waiting to see if they would hear the unexpected noise again, and after what Leaf guessed was about a minute, it did indeed happen. Leaf felt as if he had never heard a noise like it in his entire life; it was like a low howling noise or some sort of growl.

He slowly turned his head towards Selina, but her head was turned away, as she was peering through a crack to see if she could identify what was making the noise.

She couldn't see anything out of her side of the crate and she motioned her head for Leaf to try his side. Leaf turned his head and peered through a tiny crack with one eye squinting in the morning sunshine.

He could vaguely make out what he thought was another crate next to him, but that's all he could make out. He rotated his head back around the other way towards Selina, and quietly said, "Are the other three in the crate beside us on the truck?"

As the words hit Selina, her eyes narrowed in thought, as she tried to figure out if he was telling the truth or just trying to pry information out of her.

"They are leaving the ship on foot. If anyone is watching and by some slight chance manages to identify them, they will become a decoy."

"What?" Leaf blurted out loudly. "You are using my two best mates as bait?" The next voice he heard was Vicente's, and this time he spoke rather loudly in English. "Are you two, okay?"

Selina responded quickly, "*Si* Vicente. We are okay, but what is that growling noise we can hear?"

Before Vicente could respond, the low-toned growl came again from right next to them on the truck.

Vicente called back to Selina, "*Lince*."

"*Lince?* What does that even mean?" asked Leaf.

Selina yelled back to Vicente, "Really a *Lince?*"

"*Si,* a *Lince,*" yelled back Vicente quite excitedly.

Leaf had absolutely no idea what Selina or Vicente were talking about at all, when the low-pitched growl came again.

Selina then repeated herself again to Vicente. "*Lince,* really a *Lince?*"

This time, they just heard Vicente having a good laugh to himself before he put his foot on the breaks which made an ear-splitting screeching noise.

This caused whatever they were calling a *Lince* to growl even louder than earlier. Next, there were a couple of bangs on top of the create; it was Vicente signalling that it was all clear for them to get out.

Selina quickly pushed hard on the lid and removed it, and she was on her feet surveying the surrounding landscape in an instant. She looked back down at Leaf lying in the floor, and nodded to him that it was safe for him to get up.

Leaf slowly picked himself up out of the crate and looked around while stretching his body. He could see they were inside an old shed of some sort. Selina was getting out down the side of the truck, so he climbed out the other side and down next to Vicente.

It was not just Vicente though; next to him was some sort of feline sitting at attention, while Vicente stroked its head.

Selina came around the back of the truck to see them all standing there. "*Lince,* really I can't believe you brought your *Lince* with you," said Selina, shaking her head with a smile.

Leaf was still trying to put together what the other two were on about when they kept saying *Lince,* as he didn't know what the word was, though he presumed it had something to do with the feline that was next to Vicente.

Selina could tell just by looking at him that he was puzzled. "What you see there, Leaf, is Vicente's three-year-old pet Iberian Lynx. In Spanish, Lynx is pronounced *Lince*," she explained.

"Why didn't you just call it a Lynx instead of *Lince*?" asked Leaf.

Selina let out a long breath. "Leaf, you are going to have to learn other languages at some stage. You can't travel the world knowing just English," she scolded.

Leaf didn't respond to Selina's scolding, he was too busy staring at Vicente's Lynx, as he had never seen an animal like it to date. The best way to describe the Lynx was that it had a bobbed tail, a spotted coat, long legs, a muscular body, a relatively short, coarse coat, and was tawny to bright yellowish-red, with brown spots and white underparts.

"Vicente, why do you have an Iberian Lynx?" asked the ever-inquisitive Leaf.

Vicente smiled at him. "What do you know about the Iberian *Lince*, Leaf?" he asked.

Leaf just stared back blankly, shrugging his shoulders, which obvious meant 'not much.'

"The Iberian *Lince* is the rarest *Lince* species, and the most threatened cat species, and is currently on the verge of extinction," explained Vicente. "Unfortunately, they only reside in my home country of Spain and Portugal, with researchers coming to the conclusion that the population totals only around one hundred and fifty," he continued.

There was silence in the old shed, as they all found it hard to hear this sort of information about such a beautiful creature.

Leaf finally spoke. "That's awful, but that doesn't explain why you have one as a pet," he said.

Vicente smiled at Leaf again, however this time there were a couple of tears rolling down his Spanish cheeks.

"Vicente found Gato here next to his mother, who had been hit by a car on the highway," explained Selina. "One of the main reasons the Iberian Lynx is endangered, is like with so many other animals, because people are encroaching into their natural habitat."

Vicente slowly wiped away the tears from his cheeks, while with his other hand he was patting the head of his pet Lynx, Gato.

"Vicente, is it okay if I pat Gato?" asked Leaf kindly.

Vicente nodded and said, "Come over here slowly with no sudden movement. He doesn't do that well with strangers being so close to him.

Leaf slowly edged towards Gato, being careful not to make any loud noises or sudden movements, and he reached down with his hand. Luckily for everyone involved, Leaf had moved slowly enough not to spook the cat, and in turn he felt safe enough for Leaf to pat him softly on the tuffs of his furry head.

Gato seemed to be enjoying the attention.

"Well, it looks like you have made a new friend, Leaf," stated Vicente. "This is the first time I have seen Gato take to a complete stranger. It took me months to get close to him and gain his trust," he continued.

Selina hadn't spoken in a little while, and it was her turn to chime in. "It took me over a year to get close to Gato. You should feel very honoured," she said.

This comment really made Leaf think about how regularly they saw each other. In her line of work, he wouldn't have thought she would make patterns for other people to follow.

Then it suddenly dawned on him that they must be a couple. He must have a made a facial expression that caught Selina's attention as this thought crossed his mind.

"Are you okay?" she asked.

Thinking quick on his feet, he said, "I didn't think that a Lynx's fur would feel so soft," hoping that would end that conversation.

To Leaf's relief, it did, as Selina turned to speak to Vicente. "I take it that no one followed us?"

Vicente gave a swift shake of his head as an answer.

"What did you mean in the crate when you said that my friends could possibly end up being used as a decoy?" asked Leaf.

"Leaf, you seem to have a good head on your shoulders. There are going to be certain situations that you are not comfortable with. This is one of those situations," explained Selina. "Plus, you are forgetting two very important things: one, that's *if* they get recognised, and two, the most important thing is that they have Ahren there to protect them," she continued.

Leaf still felt uneasy about the situation, however he didn't want to harp on about it as they still had the pressing matter of getting to the café to find the belt buckle to deal with.

He was standing there, deep in thought about the next step, when he felt Gato rather affectionately rubbing his head against his legs, so he gave Gato a few more gentle strokes with his hand on his soft furry head.

"So, Selina, what is our next step?" he asked, now feeling eager to get to the Café. Selina switched modes from acting like a normal person to her persona of being a bodyguard.

"You three will stay in this shed while I make doubly sure we were not followed and that the area is totally secured," she stated with authority. Then she strolled over to the exit, but before she went through the door, she turned and looked at Leaf. "Don't leave this shed no matter what, okay?" she added.

THIRTY-THREE

After Selina had left, Leaf found himself with a unique opportunity to talk to Vicente one on one and gather more information about her.

He got down on his knees to be face to face with Gato and rubbed the animal's soft head, while at the same time intending to come across less like he was interrogating Vicente.

He thought he would take a subtle approach at first, to avoid Vicente getting his guard up.

"Vicente, what do you feed Gato? Isn't it difficult taking care of him seeing as you travel a lot?"

Vicente smiled back a Leaf. "It's refreshing that someone takes such an interest in him. Gato is a carnivore, so I feed him different types of meat, such as *cordera, coneja, vaca, pollo,* and sometimes, depending on the situation, he hunts for *ratona,*" he explained.

Leaf gave Vicente a blank stare, as he didn't understand what he was talking about for most of the sentence, then Vicente gave out a big bellowing laugh at the look on Leaf's befuddled face.

Leaf then gave back some sort of friendly scowl, as he didn't like being made to feel like he was dumb, and Vicente gave his short blue hair a rub with his hand. "I do my best to speak the appropriate language to a person's native tongue, however it is much easier for me to speak in Spanish," he said.

Leaf dropped the scowl as this made so much sense to him, and then he thought about what Selina had said earlier about needing to learn other languages to be a successful world traveller.

"Let me explain again," said Vicente. "*Cordera* is lamb, *coneja* is rabbit, *vaca* is beef, *pollo* is chicken, and *ratona* is mouse."

"In the back of my head I think I knew that pollo was chicken in Spanish," replied Leaf.

"Would you like to feed Gato? It's time for him to eat," said Vicente, and Leaf's face lit up with a big beaming smile and he jumped to his feet.

Vicente opened the backpack he was carrying and handed Leaf a small container, which immediately got Gato's attention, who was now walking around both of them and starting to make little growling noises.

Leaf lifted the lid off the container to find a couple of chicken breasts inside.

"Now throw them," commanded Vicente, and Leaf grabbed the chicken breasts and launched them in the air towards the other end of the old shed. Gato was immediately off like a rocket after the chicken, and just as they hit the ground, he was already ripping into them with his razor sharp teeth.

"Wow!" exclaimed Leaf. "He sure must be hungry."

"That's the way Gato always eats. I have raised him since he was small, but his animal instinct still kicks in when it's time to eat and hunt," said Vicente.

Leaf felt like it was a good time to ask some questions about Selina, since he felt like they had bonded a bit while feeding Gato. He had to choose his words wisely though, if he wanted to get some information from Vicente.

"How long have you and Selina known each other?"

"Hmm," said Vicente, rubbing his short, manicured beard. "It would be around five years, I think. Yes, five years."

"Five years. That's a fair while to know each other," replied Leaf. "How did you two meet?" he added.

"That's simple, we met each other through Ahren, of course. I had known him for a few years," answered Vicente.

Leaf might have pushed his luck too far with his line of questioning because it looked like Vicente had twigged to what he was up to.

Just then, Vicente walked away from Leaf, putting his phone to his ear and talking away in Spanish. It seemed to Leaf that he was almost having some sort of argument.

Gato came over and started rubbing up against Vicente's legs, which seemed to break up the weird tension that Leaf's questioning had brought.

In the next second, Selina came bursting through the old door, and she didn't look happy at all. She marched right past Leaf, staring him down with her eyes, as she plodded on towards Vincente, who had a worried look on his face.

Leaf figured out it must have been Selina on the other end of Vicente's phone, and by the looks of it, the arguing was going to continue.

He was right, as they started teeing off at each other quite loudly, with each one trying to talk over the top of the other in Spanish, of course. Leaf clearly did not know what they were arguing about, but he had a hunch it had to do with his question. More importantly though, he needed them to stop.

He quickly went over, placed himself in between his two friends, and threw his arms up with his hands wide open to get their full attention. His bold action caught the arguing pair off guard, and they stood there like statues, trying to compute what he was doing.

"You two need to stop this right now!" commanded Leaf. "Are you trying to draw unwanted attention to us?"

Vicente tried to hide a smirk from his face, but Selina just caught a glance of it. "You think this is funny, Vicente?" she said in a loud manner.

Leaf made a sudden movement towards Selina, which was a bold move but turned out to very stupid, because as he reached out to her, she grabbed his arm, twisted it around his back, and held him flat on his stomach on the ground.

Selina had Leaf pinned to the ground, and all he could really do was flail his legs around.

"You ever try touching me again, and I will rip your shoulder out of its socket," threatened Selina. "And also, if you keep poking around into my past, I will rip both your shoulders out of their sockets. Do you understand me, Leaf?"

"Okay, okay!" squeaked out Leaf, who was still on the ground in pain. "I will stop it."

Selina peered over towards Vicente, who took one step backwards just from her glare, feeling terrible for having given information about her away.

Vicente gave a quick sharp nod that he understood to shut his trap from now on, and Leaf pulled himself off the ground, clutching the shoulder that Selina had been wrenching on.

"I thought the idea was to be incognito and you two are yelling at each other and drawing attention to this old shed," snapped Leaf at Selina and Vincente.

They both looked rather sheepish after his comment, as they should have known better than to be so loud.

"I take it that we weren't followed, were we?" asked Leaf.

"No, we weren't followed," snapped back Selina, who was not happy with everything that had just happened.

Gato trotted over to Selina and started to rub himself up against her legs; it was like he was trying to de-escalate the situation. This seemed to work, as Selina's entire mood changed while she gave him a small pat on his little head.

"What's our next move?" questioned Leaf, but Selina just stood there silently, lighting one of her cigarettes and taking a couple of long drags.

Leaf stared blankly at her, not liking being ignored, then he went to speak again.

Selina realised this and spoke first. "What have I said about questions?" she said, taking another drag.

Leaf let out a "hmm" noise, feeling like he was about to scream in frustration, but he stopped himself and instead just kicked the ground.

Gato started moving towards Leaf; it was like he was drawn to people that were in a bad mood, but before he got there, there was a rhythmic knock on the old shed door.

Leaf and Vicente looked at each other, clueless as to what to do, then they looked over to Selina, who was making her way slowly towards door.

She opened it just slightly enough for a hand to fit through, and some keys fell into her open palm. Then, she made her way back towards the other two, and handed a key to Vicente.

"There is a white Chevrolet three blocks away to the west of here, take it, and you and Gato make your way back to the ship," she explained.

Vicente gave a small smile back to Selina as a sign that he understood her. "*Buena suerte*, Leaf," he said as he and Gato made their way to the shed door.

Leaf had no idea what Vicente had just said, however he got the distinct feeling that he wouldn't be seeing him any time soon. "Thank you for your help," he said.

Vicente and Gato left the shed and Leaf turned to Selina.

"What he said was good luck," explained Selina, beating Leaf to the punch, as she grabbed her phone from her pocket and took a quick glance at it. "In ten minutes, if nothing happens, we will walk east two blocks to a Vesper," she said.

Leaf gave a perplexed look back towards his protector. "Nope. For the bloody hundredth time, no more questions!" barked Selina. "We will wait here in silence."

Leaf looked like he was going to blow up at Selina, with his cheeks all puffed up like a puffer fish or a chipmunk's mouth full of nuts. However, he managed to stop himself from screaming again, as he didn't want to draw any unwanted attention.

THIRTY-FOUR

Meanwhile, way back at the oil tanker, Leaf's two mates were only just waking up, and they were not sure what was going on as they both realised Leaf and Selina were not in the cabin.

Ahren was standing guard at the exit and he immediately explained, "They have already left the ship."

Summo and Spence were lost for words. They knew they would be going their separate ways, but they had expected to be able to say goodbye.

"Mr. Summers and Mr. Blake, you have two minutes to get yourselves organised before we depart," commanded Ahren.

The two mates frantically grabbed what they had out and stuffed it into their bags, while Ahren waited by the door tapping his finger. The mates were ready to roll in under two minutes and were standing next to Ahren waiting to leave.

As they made their way off the ship, Summo and Spence exchanged worried glances. They did not know where Leaf and Selina had gone, and they had a sinking feeling that they wouldn't be seeing their friend any time soon.

Ahren led them to a waiting car and quickly got into the driver's seat, starting up the engine and pulling out onto the road. The drive was filled with silence, the tension palpable between the three men. Summo and Spence couldn't help but speculate on what could have possibly happened to Leaf, while Ahren kept his eyes trained on the road ahead, his face unreadable.

Finally, they arrived at their destination: a small hotel tucked away in a quiet corner of the city. Ahren led them inside and up to a room on the second floor, opening the door and gesturing for them to enter.

As soon as they were inside, Ahren turned to them and spoke in a no-nonsense tone. "Listen up, gentlemen. We don't have much time. The area has been compromised and we need to move fast. I have orders to get you two out of the country as soon as possible."

Summo and Spence exchanged worried glances once again, wondering what had gone wrong.

"What about Leaf?" asked Spence, unable to contain his concern any longer.

Ahren's face remained stoic. "Leaf is no longer our concern. We've had to part ways for the time being."

Summo and Spence looked at each other in shock, not quite understanding what Ahren meant by "parting ways."

Ahren continued, "We have new identities for you both and flights booked for tonight. You will both be flying out separately to different destinations. Once you have landed, you will receive further instructions on what to do next."

Summo and Spence nodded in agreement, still reeling from Leaf's absence.

Ahren handed them each a new passport and other documents, instructing them to memorise their new identities.

"You must keep a low profile and blend in. Do not draw any attention to yourselves," warned Ahren. With that, he left the room, leaving Summo and Spence to process what had just happened.

They sat in silence for a few moments, before Summo spoke up. "What do you think happened to Leaf?"

Spence shook his head. "I don't know, but it can't be good if they had to separate him from us."

They spent the next few hours preparing for their flights, going over their new identities, and practicing their cover stories.

As they packed their bags, they couldn't help but wonder what would happen once they landed in their new destinations. Would they ever see Leaf again?

The fact is that they were not in imminent danger, but what the two mates didn't realise, is that this was part of Ahren and Selina's plan to get them out of the country and solely focus on Leaf.

Meanwhile, Selina and Leaf were still waiting in the shed, the silence between them suffocating. Leaf was getting restless, his mind wandering to all the plausible scenarios that could be playing out.

Selina remained calm and collected, her focus on the task at hand. Finally, Selina broke the silence. "It's time to go," she said, extinguishing her cigarette and standing up.

Leaf followed suit, and they made their way out of the shed, cautiously looking around for any signs of danger.

They walked for a few blocks in silence, with Selina purposefully leading the way. Leaf couldn't help but notice the way she moved; she was so confident of herself. He wondered how she had become so skilled in the art of espionage.

Finally, they arrived at their destination: a small Vespa parked outside a run-down building.

Selina turned to Leaf and said, "Get on the bike. We're heading to the safe house."

Leaf nodded, his heart pounding with anticipation as he climbed onto the Vespa behind Selina. They sped off into the night, weaving in and out of traffic as they made their way through the city. Leaf held onto Selina tightly, trying to keep his nerves at bay as he watched the chaos of the city pass by.

After what felt like an eternity, they finally arrived at a small apartment building on the outskirts of the city. Selina parked the Vespa and led Leaf inside, up a flight of stairs, and into a small, one-bedroom apartment.

"This is where we'll be staying for the time being," Selina said, looking around the small space with a critical eye.

"Make yourself at home, but don't get too comfortable, we'll be moving again soon."

Leaf nodded, still trying to take everything in. He didn't know how to feel. He wanted to ask Selina more questions; to understand what was going on, but he knew better than to push her.

Instead, he took a seat on the small couch and tried to relax. As he sat there, his mind began to wander. He had always dreamed of adventure and excitement, but he never imagined it would be like this. He thought of his friends Summo and Spence, and wondered where they were and if they were okay. He also couldn't help but think about his family back home, wondering if they were worried about him or even knew he was gone.

As his thoughts drifted; he was interrupted by Selina's voice.

"We need to talk," she said, taking a seat next to him on the couch. Leaf nervously shifted in his seat, unsure of what was coming next.

"What is it?" he asked. Selina took a deep breath before speaking. "I need to tell you the truth about Summo and Spence."

Leaf's heart rate quickened as he waited for her to continue.

"They're safe, but they had to leave the country immediately. We couldn't risk them getting caught up in the situation anymore."

Leaf's mind raced as he tried to process this information.

Why did they have to leave? What situation?" he asked, his voice barely above a whisper.

It was my decision to split you all up," Selina explained. "We needed to focus solely on you, Leaf."

Leaf's facial expression changed; he was not a happy camper at having been kept out of loop, especially seeing as he was the one outlaying all the money, and this was his journey.

He felt a mix of anger and betrayal, wondering why no one had consulted him before making such a drastic decision.

"It was bad enough you split us up on the tanker, and now they're getting shipped off to who knows where!" yelled an annoyed Leaf.

Selina held up her hand to calm him down. "I know this is a lot to take in, but we had to act quickly."

Leaf shook his head, still frustrated by the lack of communication. "I understand that, but I should have been informed. I'm not a child, Selina. I can handle the truth."

Selina nodded. "You're right, we should have told you sooner."

Leaf took a deep breath, trying to calm himself down. He knew that

Selina was only trying to help, but he couldn't shake the feeling of being left in the dark.

"Okay," he said finally. "What's the plan now?"

THIRTY-FIVE

"Summo and Spence will be flown out in the next few hours to separate countries. They'll be escorted by Ahren to the planes, then he will rendezvous with us here," explained Selina calmly, trying to keep Leaf at ease.

"What about us?" Leaf asked.

"As I said just before, we wait for Ahren then we discuss our next move to the café," responded Selina.

Leaf nodded, feeling a bit better now that he knew the plan. He knew he had to trust Selina and Ahren, even if he didn't always agree with their methods.

As they waited for Ahren to arrive, Leaf couldn't help but think about his friends. He hoped they were safe and that they would be reunited soon. He also couldn't shake the feeling that there was more to the situation than what he had been told.

Meanwhile, in another part of Havana, Summo and Spence were trying to get their heads around the situation, while they were getting ready to be whisked away to an unknown destination.

They were sat in a dingy hotel room, their bags packed and ready to go. Summo paced back and forth, his mind racing with questions and worries.

"Do you think Leaf is okay?" he asked for the hundredth time.

Spence sighed, trying to remain calm and collected.

"I'm sure he's fine. Ahren and Selina wouldn't have let anything happen to him."

Summo nodded, but he couldn't shake the feeling of unease. As they waited for Ahren to arrive and take them to the airport, they tried to distract themselves by going over their new identities and practicing their cover stories. The tension in the air was palpable, and neither of them could fully relax. Finally, there was a knock on the door and Ahren entered the room. "It's time to go Mr. Summer and Mr. Blake," he said.

Summo and Spence grabbed their bags and followed Ahren out of the hotel room and into a waiting car. They drove through the streets of Havana in silence, each lost in their own thoughts and worries.

As they arrived at the airport, Ahren handed them their passports and fake IDs again. "Remember, stick to your cover stories and don't draw attention to yourselves," he warned before sending them off to their separate flights.

As the two mates made their way through the terminal, Spence asked Summo, "Where are they sending you?"

Summo went through his pocket and pulled out the ticket. "I am going to Balboa in Panama," he said.

Then he looked at his mate and asked, "What about you?"

Spence gave a cheeky grin back to his mate.

"Oh, come on, don't tell me your country is better than mine?" moaned Summo.

"I am going to Trinidad and Tobago," announced Spence gladly.

They went their separate ways, feeling a mix of relief and sadness as they parted. They knew that they had to keep their guard up and stick to their cover stories, but they couldn't shake the sad feeling from being separated from their friend Leaf and the uncertainty of what was to come.

Meanwhile, back at the safe house, Leaf was still waiting for Ahren to arrive. He paced back and forth, his mind racing with questions and worries.

Finally, he heard a knock on the door and Selina went to answer it. Ahren entered the room, looking as stoic as ever.

"I've secured a new safe house for us," he said, "but we need to hurry."

Leaf grabbed his backpack and followed Selina and Ahren out of the small apartment and into the bustling streets of Havana. They moved quickly, blending in with the crowds and trying to avoid drawing attention to themselves. Leaf couldn't help but feel a little envious of the normalcy of the surrounding people, walking to work or chatting with friends.

He wondered what it would be like to live a life without all the danger and uncertainty that seemed to follow him everywhere.

As they arrived at the new safe house, Leaf couldn't help but feel a sense of relief wash over him. The building was small but clean and well-appointed, with comfortable beds and a modern kitchen. Selina and Ahren quickly got to work fortifying the perimeter and setting up surveillance equipment.

Leaf watched in awe as they worked, marvelling at how well-trained and efficient they were. After they finished setting up, it was Leaf's chance to strike and ask some questions that had been swirling around in his head.

"Okay, enough with the secrets and half-truths. What is really going on here?" Leaf demanded. Selina and Ahren exchanged a look before turning to face Leaf.

"Mr. Brodie, I received intel that Tamina has called in reinforcements to track us down, so I made the decision to split the group as it would be harder for them to find us," explained Ahren.

Leaf took a deep breath as he let the information sink into his brain. "Where did you send Summo and Spence, and are they safe?" he asked.

"They've been flown out to separate countries with new identities so they won't be easily tracked," answered Selina swiftly.

Leaf raised both eyebrows in frustration. "Which countries?" he snapped back.

Selina was getting frustrated as she hated getting asked questions. "Summo has been sent to Panama and Spence is going to Trinidad and Tobago," she replied.

Leaf nodded, feeling a mix of relief and sadness at the news. He was glad to hear that his friends were safe, but he couldn't shake off the sad feeling at being separated from them.

"What do we do now?" he asked, turning to face Selina and Ahren.

"Well, Mr. Brodie, you will stay here in this safe house while we do some recon work on the café and surroundings," replied Ahren.

Leaf let out a slight sigh of disappointment, but Ahren and Selina just ignored it, as they didn't want to keep going back and forth with questions and answers.

"Leaf, why don't you find a room and settle yourself in?" suggested Selina.

Leaf trudged off to find a room, feeling disappointed that he would be cooped up inside and couldn't get some fresh air by himself.

He selected a room and lay down on the bed, reflecting on what had been a crazy day when he stopped to think about it.

Being whisked away in a crate, meeting an Iberian Lynx, having his two mates sent away, and finding out there was more danger in store as Reblick reinforcements were coming to Cuba.

He wondered what would happen next, and whether he would be able to keep himself and his friends safe. No matter how hard he tried, he couldn't shake off the feeling of being alone. He missed his friends and wished that they were there with him.

He knew he had to trust Selina and Ahren, but he couldn't help but feel a sense of apprehension about what was to come. He decided to get out the book that had started this somewhat crazy journey, so he could make sure he hadn't missed anything important.

While reading, he started to yawn frequently, as it had been a long day mentally. After more reading and yawning, Leaf's eyes finally gave in and closed off to sleep.

"Mr. Brodie, it's time to eat," Ahren's voice came through the door.

Leaf groaned, feeling more tired than hungry, but he knew he needed to keep up his strength if he wanted to stay sharp and alert.

He got up slowly and made his way to the dining room. Selina and Ahren were already there, sitting at the table and chatting quietly. They looked up when Leaf entered the room, and Selina smiled warmly at him.

"Sit down and eat, Mr. Brodie," said Ahren, gesturing towards the food on the table. Leaf sat down and grabbed a plate, feeling grateful for the warm meal. As they ate, they talked about their next steps and the scenarios they might encounter.

Leaf tried to listen carefully, so he could be as prepared as possible, but he was still yawning a lot and feeling groggy. He struggled to take in what Selina and Ahren were discussing. They were mid-sentence, when Leaf suddenly got up and announced, "I need a shower to wake up so I know what is going on," and he made his way to the bathroom.

He turned on the shower, feeling the hot water wash over his tired body, and he closed his eyes, letting out a sigh of relief, the stress and tension from the past few days melting away.

It felt like days since he'd had a shower, and he always did enjoy a long warm shower to help him unwind. As he finished up, he dried off and got dressed into some fresh clothes. Then he made his way back to the dining room, feeling more awake and alert.

Selina and Ahren were still there, discussing their plan of action for the next few days.

"Okay, I'm ready," Leaf announced as he sat down at the table.

"Let's go over the plan again." Selina and Ahren exchanged a look before beginning to explain the plan once more.

THIRTY-SIX

Selina gave a slight stare at Leaf before she spoke. "We have located Café el Runika, and we can confirm that it was owned by Nila Runika. The place is still located in its original building, and it is still kept within the family."

Leaf listened to Selina intently, then he suddenly thought about the possibility that he was wrong about the place. He was just going off some basic Google research he'd done, and it happened to be the only match. What were the odds that this was where he was supposed to be?

His train of thought was interrupted by Selina. "The café is run by Elana, who handles the kitchen, and her daughter, Marta, who takes care of the front of the house."

"There are a few things that make our mission a little complicated, Mr. Brodie," chimed in Ahren. "Elana, the mother, is almost never seen in public, and there are no records kept on the house."

The information flowed over Leaf. "Hmm, so let me get this straight: we don't know the identity of the person who may have the answers I need?"

"Correct," replied Selina.

"And no records means not knowing how many entry or exit points there are."

"Correct," said Selina again.

"Why did you call it a house when speaking about the plans?" asked Leaf.

"It is very common that people use their house as a place of business, in this case a café," explained Ahren.

"Oh," said Leaf, finding this concept quite foreign.

"The last point Ahren made is very important. Being off the beaten track, as you may put it, means that Reblick would be willing to take more chances," said Selina.

Leaf nodded, still trying to fully grasp the situation.

"From the information we have gathered, the best time to go there is around two o'clock, as it is normally a slower part of the day," explained Ahren.

"So, what's the plan once we get there?" asked Leaf, looking at Selina and Ahren.

"We'll have to be discreet," replied Selina. "We don't want to attract any unwanted attention."

"Mr. Brodie and Miss Delacruise will be separate customers in the café, as I watch from the building across the street. That way we have two excellent vantage points to watch out for Reblick while making sure you are safe," explained Ahren.

"Once we are in there," followed up Selina, "you will talk to Martha and hopefully get the information you need."

"What would be the best way to do that?" asked Leaf keenly.

"That will be up to you, Mr. Brodie, as you will have to be yourself to gain their trust," explained Ahren, whose German accent was becoming more familiar to him.

Leaf sucked in a big breath of air. "When are we going to the café?" he enquired.

"Tomorrow afternoon, Leaf," responded Selina.

"The sooner we get the information you require, the sooner we can get you out," said Ahren, standing up. The big German's hulking shadow engulfed the table. "We all have to prepare for tomorrow. I suggest we get some rest," he added.

Selina stood up and followed her mentor's lead, so she was sure she would be ready for whatever tomorrow may bring.

Leaf couldn't shake the feeling of nervousness that was building up inside him. He knew that tomorrow was going to be a crucial day, and he knew he had to try his best to get the information he needed.

With that in mind, he made his way to his bedroom and got ready for bed. As he lay there, his mind raced with thoughts of what tomorrow might bring. He tried to calm himself down by taking deep breaths and counting backwards from ten, but the more he tried to relax, the more his mind kept returning to the possibilities of what could happen.

He couldn't help but think about the danger they might face.

What if they were caught? What if Reblick found out about their plan? What if he never got the answers he was looking for?

Leaf felt a sense of dread wash over him as he thought about the worst-case scenarios, but he knew that he couldn't let his fear hold him back. He had come too far to turn back now.

He closed his eyes and tried to focus on the present moment, thinking about the warmth of the bed beneath him, the softness of the pillow under his head, and the sound of his own breath as it moved in and out of his body.

Slowly but surely, this calmed him down and he drifted off to sleep.

As he slept, Leaf's dreams were filled with images of the café, Reblick, and the mysterious answers he was searching for. He tossed and turned in his bed, his mind unable to rest even in his dreams. But amidst the chaos, there was one image that stood out to him. It was a woman with long, flowing hair and piercing green eyes.

She was standing in the doorway of the café, watching him with a mixture of curiosity and suspicion. Leaf couldn't explain why, but he felt drawn to her. He wanted to know who she was and what she knew. As he slept, the woman's image grew stronger and more vivid. He could see every detail of her face – the curve of her lips, the freckles on her nose, the way her hair fell in loose curls around her shoulders.

Then suddenly, he was jolted awake by the sound of a loud crash. He sat up in bed, heart racing, and listened intently for any more signs of danger. But there was nothing. Just the sound of his own breathing and the faint hum of the city outside his window. He lay back down, trying to calm his racing heart.

Just as he was about to drift off to sleep again, he heard a faint knock at the door. He sat up, heart racing once more, and listened intently.

Another knock followed, a little louder this time. Who could be knocking at his door, he wondered.

He got out of bed and slowly made his way there, trying to stay as quiet as possible. As he reached for the doorknob, he couldn't help but feel a sense of unease.

What if it was Reblick? What if he had already been caught? But he couldn't just stay in his room and ignore the knocking either. Taking a deep breath, he opened the door to reveal a figure standing in the hallway. It was his protector, Selina.

"Rise and shine, it's time to get ready for the day."

Leaf rubbed his sleepy eyes. "Is it morning already? I'll get dressed right away," he replied.

He quickly put on his clothes and met Selina and Ahren in the living room, where they discussed the plan again, going over every detail to make sure they were all on the same page.

As they prepared to leave, Leaf felt a surge of nervousness once again, but he pushed it aside and reminded himself that he had to be brave.

They made their way to the café, with Ahren taking his position across the street, while Leaf entered the building.

The café was small and cozy, with the smell of fresh coffee and baked goods filling the air. Leaf just sat there, taking everything in, then Selina entered, finding a table only a few meters behind him.

Leaf peered around the picturesque building, and his eyes caught something – or more to the point, someone – standing behind the front counter. The person looked familiar. Even more so after the afternoon sun filtered through a small window to reveal the woman from his dream last night.

Leaf blinked a few times, rubbing his eyes. He couldn't believe what he was seeing. He could see her deep auburn hair and piercing green eyes in the sunlight. He stared at her, mesmerised, as she moved gracefully around the café, serving customers and chatting with them.

He knew he had to talk to her, so he stood up, took a deep breath, and made his way to the counter. "Excuse me," he said, trying to keep his voice steady. "I was wondering if you could help me."

The woman turned to him, a faint smile on her lips. "Of course," she said. "What do you need?"

Leaf swallowed hard, feeling his nerves getting the best of him. "I'm looking for someone," he said.

The woman's smile faded slightly, and she looked at him with a hint of suspicion.

"Someone?" she repeated. "Normally people will ask me for a recommendation on what to eat or drink," answered Marta. Leaf was taken aback by this response, but also by the way she spoke clear and concise English. He didn't have to respond however, as the woman from his dream asked, "Who is this person you are looking for?"

"Marta," he replied.

The woman's expression changed, and she looked at him warily. "Why do you want to find Marta?" she asked, her eyes narrowing.

"I just need to speak with her," Leaf replied, trying to keep his tone calm and neutral.

She studied him for a moment then nodded slowly. "I see," she said. "Well, I am Marta. What do you want to talk to me about?"

Leaf felt a rush of relief mixed with nerves. "You're Marta," he blurted out. "You're the women from my dream."

Marta took a couple of quick steps back from the counter, the words having spooked her.

"What?" she said sharply. "What do you mean, you dreamed of me?"

Leaf took a step back, feeling the weight of her gaze upon him. "I... I don't know," he stammered. "It was just a dream. I saw you and I felt drawn to you. I didn't mean to make you uncomfortable."

"Is this some random pick-up line you use on different women?" Marta questioned.

"No, no, no," repeated Leaf, feeling rather foolish revealing his dream to her. "I didn't mean it like that."

Marta's expression softened slightly. "I see," she said. "Well, I'm sorry if I seemed rude. It's just that I don't really know you, and it's strange to have someone say they dreamed about you."

Leaf could feel the tension in the air between the two of them, and also Selina staring a hole through the back of his head. He decided to introduce himself properly in hope it would ease the situation.

"Anyway, my name is Leaf," he said in a cheerful voice, raising his right hand out for a handshake.

Marta hesitated for a moment, then shook his hand tentatively. "Nice to meet you, Leaf," she said, a faint smile on her lips. "I'm sorry if I seemed suspicious earlier. It's just that these days, you never know who you can trust."

Leaf nodded, understanding her caution. "I get it," he said. "But I promise I'm not here to cause any trouble. I just need to ask you a few questions."

Marta looked at him for a moment, then nodded slowly. "Okay," she said. "What do you want to know?"

Leaf took a deep breath, gathering his thoughts. "I was wondering," he said, "how long have you owned this café?"

Marta's expression relaxed a bit, and she leaned against the counter. "It has been in my family for as long as I can remember," she said with a big smile across her face. "I run it with my mama."

Leaf smiled back, feeling a warmth spread inside of him. "That's amazing," he said. "It must be great to have something like that to share with your family."

Marta nodded, a wistful look in her eyes. "Yes," she said. "It's been a rough year, but we're managing. We're lucky to have each other."

Leaf could sense a sadness in her voice and wondered what had made it a rough year. "Is everything okay?" he asked, hoping he wasn't overstepping any boundaries.

Marta hesitated for a moment before answering. "It's nothing too serious," she said with a shrug. "Just some financial difficulties, but we're managing, like I said."

After hearing Marta talk, it gave him an idea how he could get the answer he required, but that would also benefit Marta and her mama.

"Is it possible that we can have a private conversation somewhere else?" asked Leaf with a friendly smile beaming across his face.

Marta looked hesitant about the idea.

"There is a lot for me to do here," she replied, but Leaf wasn't going to give up that easily. "How about I pay for your time to answer my questions? That way, hopefully that can help you and your mama with the café," he said, trying to sound persuasive.

Marta didn't feel that comfortable about being in a room by herself with someone she had only just met, however the money would help. "I will answer your questions, but we will do it here at a table in a quiet corner of the café."

Leaf was about to respond, but Marta cut him off. "That is the only way," she said sternly.

Leaf paused for a second to think about this, and a couple of things went through his mind. Would Reblick be watching him? Would he be safe? And then he remembered that he had Selina and Ahren looking out for him.

Leaf smiled as he gave a quick nod in agreeance to Marta's wishes, and she led him over to a table in a quiet part of the café where there were no other customers.

Before they sat down, Marta stopped herself. "Where are my manners? Is there anything you want?"

This caught Leaf off guard. "Um, yeah... no," he managed to mumble back.

THIRTY-SEVEN

Marta smiled and gestured for him to sit down, and as they took their seats, Leaf couldn't help but feel a sense of excitement mixed with nerves.

He had a feeling that Marta might hold the key, but he didn't want to get his hopes up too high. "So, what do you want to know?" Marta asked, folding her hands on the table.

Leaf took a deep breath, trying to focus. "Well, to be honest," he began, "this is going to sound crazy, but please bear with me."

Marta squinted her eyes at him, as this was a very odd way to start a conversation, so Leaf decided he would come straight out with the hard questions first, to see if he could catch her off-guard so she would give something away.

He spoke very directly to Marta. "I need you to tell me absolutely everything about the country Xonarye."

Marta's face sort of screwed up with a sense of confusion.

"Um, where now?" she slowly said.

"Xonarye. X-o-n-a-r-y-e," spelt out Leaf very slowly and precisely.

Marta looked at him for a moment before responding. "I'm sorry, I'm not sure what you're talking about," she said. "I've never heard of that place before."

Leaf felt like she was telling the truth, but he needed some answers somehow. He decided to take a gamble and reveal to her the old book. He handed it to Marta and asked, "Do you read English?"

"Yes, I can read English well enough, but I still don't understand," answered a confused Marta.

Leaf took a deep breath and began to explain. "This book is ancient, and it talks about a country called Xonarye. It's a hidden country, and I believe that it might hold the key to finding this lost country."

Marta looked at the book sceptically. "I'm not sure I understand," she said. "What does this have to do with me?"

Leaf leaned forward, looking Marta directly in the eyes. "I have a clue that has brought me here."

"I'm sorry, Leaf," she said. "But I really don't know anything about this place you speak of."

Leaf put his hands over his face in frustration. Surely, this wasn't a dead end. An idea suddenly popped into his mind. "Can I talk to your mama about this?" he asked cautiously.

"Excuse me," responded Marta quite abruptly.

"Name the price and I will pay," said Leaf, quick as whip.

Marta said something, and Leaf wasn't sure if it was to him or she was saying it to herself. "*Qué barbaridad!*"

As Leaf didn't speak Spanish, he was unsure what to do or say, so he just sat in silence waiting for her response. Finally, Marta let out a deep sigh and looked at him.

"Okay," she said hesitantly. "I'll talk to my mother about it, but I can't promise anything. And I expect to be paid for my time."

Leaf let out a sigh of relief. At least he had made some progress. "Thank you, Marta," he said with a grateful smile. "I appreciate it. Just let me know when she's available."

Marta nodded and stood up. "I'll let you know," she said, before walking back behind the counter.

Leaf watched Marta walk away feeling relieved that she had agreed to talk to her mother. He knew that he was one step closer to finding the next clue to Xonarye, and he couldn't wait to see what Marta's mother would say about it.

He decided to stay in the café for a while longer, ordering a coffee to pass the time. Just then, Marta came back over to his table. "My mother will see you now," she said, gesturing for Leaf to follow her. Leaf got up from the table and followed Marta out the back to the kitchen.

There sat a large elderly lady at an old wooden table with finely braided hair put up in a hairstyle that Leaf had never seen nor knew how to describe.

"This is Leaf, Mama. The man I told you about," announced Marta.

Marta's mum Elana sat there looking at Leaf, sizing him up. In a soft tone voice, she spoke very slowly in English. "My daughter tells me you are looking for information that is lost."

"Yes, ma'am, I am looking for information on a lost country called Xonarye," explained Leaf.

"Tell me Leaf, where are you from?" asked Elana in her soft tone. It was clearly how she normally spoke.

"I am from Australia," answered Leaf, who was unsure why she was asking.

"Do you know about your heritage?" asked Elana.

"I understand a little; my parents have spoken to me about it, but I haven't really taken much interest," explained Leaf.

Elana pursed he lips then asked another question. "Tell me what you know about Cuba?"

"Mama, why are you asking these questions?" interrupted her daughter, who, like Leaf, wasn't sure where she was going with this.

Elana waved her right hand at her daughter, showing her to leave the kitchen. Marta wanted to protest, but her mum glared at her.

"Can you answer my question please, boy?" repeated Elana.

"Um, yes ma'am," replied Leaf, who was starting to feel a bit uneasy and unsure about the situation he found himself in. The old lady just sat there unmoved and spoke so quietly, but she had an aura of authority that demanded respect.

Leaf took a deep breath to compose himself before he spoke. "Cuba is a country in the Caribbean sea, the language is Spanish, the capital is Havana, the currency is the peso, and Fidel Castro led a revolution."

Elana shook her head. This was the first time she had shown any type of body language. "You know nothing, you have just read the information from a book," said Elana, who looked disappointed with Leaf's answer.

She continued, "Cuba, like all countries, isn't made up by those things or held together by boundaries, oceans, or politics. What makes a country, any country, is the people… the people who live here now, were here before, and who are to come."

Elana gave a small cough into her hand before continuing. "The Indigenous people of Cuba were called the *Taíno* people, since then Cuba has had many people come from multiple backgrounds: Spanish, Africans, French, Chinese, Italians, Haitians; these are the nationalities that have migrated to Cuba over the centuries. These diverse cultures have contributed to the unique and vibrant cultural identity of the Cuban people. Don't you understand that these people from all over the globe make up countries in their own unique way, not the words you used before that you have recited from a book?"

Leaf was baffled with what was going on. He had no idea what Elana was talking about, but he knew he had just been told off. Elana then leaned forward and looked him in the eyes. "If you really want to find Xonarye, you must understand that it's not just about finding a lost country. It's about understanding the people and their culture. You cannot just read books and expect to find what you're looking for. You must immerse yourself in the culture and learn from the people who live there. There is wonder and amazement all about you, like beautiful music, and you stand there stiff with no rhythm."

Leaf was getting annoyed. He was being told off in the most bizarre way, and it felt like she was talking in some type of weird riddle.

He looked at Elana, who was just staring at him like she was waiting for him to figure out what she was talking about.

He started to pace in the kitchen back and forth thinking about the old lady's words while she watched him and waited for a response.

She cleared her throat. "The longer you take, the more pesos you give to my family."

Leaf couldn't figure out what was going on and it must have showed on his face, because for the first time, Elana raised her voice. "*Idiota.*"

Leaf was quite startled by her tone. "I have been talking about people Leaf, where they are from, what their background is," explained Elana.

"I understand that," said Leaf, trying to keep his frustration in check. "But what does that have to do with finding Xonarye?"

"Me, my family, and my ancestors have been waiting, waiting, so, so long for this day to come," said Elana with some cracking in her voice, as a couple of tears dropped down her cheek.

"You are looking to find this country, and me, like the rest of my family, are trying to find our past; who we are, what we did, and everything," said an emotional Elana.

It finally dawned on Leaf what was going on; she was looking for answers just like he was, only different ones.

"Your ancestors were from Xonarye, weren't they?" asked Leaf.

More tears spilled down the old lady's cheeks. "I-I have never told a soul that before," she cried. She put her left hand out, palm up, and Leaf placed the old book he had found in the old farm house that had started this journey, in her hand.

Elana clutched it tight, like a long-lost treasure or family member, as she continued to cry.

Leaf felt a mix of emotions as Elana cried. He had never thought that his search for Xonarye would be connected to someone else's personal history in such a profound way.

He felt a sense of responsibility to help her find the answers she was searching for, just as he was searching for his own answers.

He sat down next to Elana. "How about you read this book? It will give you some of the answers you are looking for," said Leaf with a smile.

Elana gave half a smile back. She was filled with so much emotion right now, she was finding it very difficult to control.

She wiped away the tears from her leaking eyes with the sleeves of her jumper. "Can you help me please?" she asked. "My reading of English is not very good."

"It would be my pleasure," answered Leaf, who was more than happy to help Elana and her family find out about their past.

The two sat there for about an hour, as Elana, with Leaf's help, read the book about Xonarye. Marta came in to check what was going on with them, and ten minutes later, Selina strolled into the kitchen too, with Marta right behind her, yelling at her in Spanish then English.

"You can't be back here!"

"It's okay, Marta," said Leaf to defuse the situation. "She is with me."

Marta looked at her mama, who nodded back, and with that she left the kitchen.

"I am very lucky to have her as my daughter, she is strong willed and takes great care of me. One day I hope she will find a husband to help her run this café," said Elana.

"Elana, this is my friend Selina. Selina, this is Elana, her ancestors are from Xonarye," explained Leaf.

Selina surveyed the room, taking in every little detail. "Where are you with the information you need?" she asked.

"We are getting there, aren't we Elana?" answered Leaf, as he smiled at the old lady, who smiled back.

Selina had an intense look on her face. "You can take a seat over there in the corner if you like," suggested Elana.

"How about I fetch us a pot of *Té Negro*," said Elana, as she went over to the sink and filled up an old teapot. She placed the teapot on the open flame of the stove, and Leaf presumed that *Té Negro* was tea.

As Elana brewed the tea, Selina took a seat in the corner of the kitchen. Elana brought over the pot of *Té Negro* and three cups, and poured a cup for each of them. Leaf took a sip; it was strong and bitter, but he liked it.

As they drank their tea, Leaf and Elana went back to going through the book together. The hours passed as they read the book and discussed unique elements of Xonarye, while Selina sat in the corner and waited.

As the sun began to set, Elana closed the book and let out a deep sigh. "It's all so much to take in," she said, looking exhausted. Leaf could see the weight of the information she had just digested on her face.

"How do you feel after that, Elana?"

Elana signed. "Tried, emotional, relieved. There is a lot of information to take in and understand."

Leaf reached into one of his pockets and placed some coins on the top of the old wooden table. It was the Xped coins, the currency of Xonarye.

Elana stared at the odd shaped silver currency. "Is it really Xped?" she asked.

"Yes," affirmed Leaf. "And before you ask, they are made of Xzed."

Elana leaned over and slowly picked up a couple of coins, smiling at Leaf with happy eyes. "Leaf, you have made this very old Mama happy, you know?" she said.

"It's now my turn to share my family secret with you." Elana put her hands in her braided hair, and it forced Selina into action, as she leapt off her chair onto the table and grabbed Elana's arms before she could bring them back out of her hair.

Leaf just stared at Selina, while Elana was completely frozen in shock by her behaviour.

"Tell me what's in your hair?" barked Selina loudly.

Elana didn't respond; she was just frozen and staring back at her.

Selina's gaze turned to Leaf. "You are going to get whatever she is reaching for and bring it out slowly."

"W-w-what?" stammered Leaf, who didn't feel comfortable about what was going on, nor putting his hands in someone else's hair.

Elana must have come around to Selina's shock move, as she calmly said, "It's okay Leaf, do as your friend asks."

Leaf gulped as he carefully reached into Elana's braided hair; he had never felt braids before, and it was an unusual texture against his skin.

His hand felt something soft, and as he grasped for the item, it suddenly felt a lot harder. He slowly brough it out of Elana's web of hair to reveal a tattered white brownish cloth that was wrapped around something.

Elana very calmy asked Selina, "May I show the item to you?"

Selina let go of the old lady's arms and climbed down off the old wooden table. Leaf hand the package over to Elana, who had a wry grin on her face. "This is my secret and I believe what you are looking for."

Elana placed the cloth bundle on the table, and with her wrinkly fingers, carefully unwrapped the discoloured material.

As she unfolded the last bit of it, there sat the belt buckle, identical to the one Leaf had found in the old house back in his hometown.

Leaf stood up and removed the belt strapped around his waist, laying it down next to the buckle on the table. Then he picked up both buckles, one in each hand, spinning them around and examining them closely. "They look identical," he announced. "Elana, do you have something heavy I can hit the buckle with?" asked Leaf.

She strolled over to draw and pulled out a large meat tenderizer, while the whole time Selina was eyeballing the old lady.

Leaf grabbed the large tenderizer and gave Elana's buckle two quick stiff hard whacks. Selina sat there unmoved by Leaf's actions, however it caused a little gasp to escape Elana's mouth.

He picked up the buckle and scrutinised it, then a giant smile beamed across the young Australians face. "It's real. It's real!" bellowed Leaf in glee, as he jumped up and down holding the buckle high in the air.

Selina stood up and gazed at the two belt buckles, then she picked up the cloth and flipped it over on both sides. "Were is the clue?"

Leaf and Selina turned to Elana, both of them hoping for an answer. "This is all I have," replied the old lady, as the three of them stood there in the kitchen of a café around an old wooden table, dumbfounded, looking at two silver belt buckles and a tattered discoloured cloth.

9 781763 605909